SILVER VALLEY

Bert Lomax thought the discovery of silver in the valley would do the town a heap of good. But Brad Fulsom and Matt Glass had other ideas and stole some of the silver and hid it in an old mine. After getting involved with Isabel Forrester, her father made things worse by having the Murraghs killed, which brought Jed Guthrie to town. Before long the scene was set for a bloody showdown when justice was meted out with hot lead.

Ber
in t
goo
had
and
inv
ma
kill
Bef
sho
witl

SILVER VALLEY

SILVER VALLEY

by

H. H. Cody

Dales Large Print Books
Long Preston, North Yorkshire, England.

British Library Cataloguing in Publication Data.

Cody, H.H.
Silver valley

A catalogue record for this book is
available from the British Library

ISBN 1-85389-950-X pbk

First published in Great Britain by Robert Hale Ltd., 1998

Published in Large Print 1999 by arrangement with Robert
Hale Ltd.

Dales Large Print is an imprint of
Library Magna Books Ltd.
Printed and bound in Great Britain by
T.J. International Ltd., Cornwall, PL28 8RW.

One

The foliage of the trees was so dense in the Colorado Valley that the sun had trouble getting through. Only here and there did it splash the dusty trail. The scenic beauty of the valley was lost on Abe Keller as he raised the whiskey bottle to his thick lips and swallowed deeply. The fiery liquid burned the back of his throat.

'Gonna keep a mouthful for me?' Milt Drew called as he rode a few yards behind Keller on the narrow trail.

'Aw, keep your wind,' replied Keller turning and waiting for his amigo. Taking the bottle Drew drank as deeply as Keller had done, then belched loudly.

'Keep makin' that much noise, an' Murtagh's gonna be hearin' you in hell,' complained Keller, relieving Drew of the bottle.

'Wal, it's the last thing he's gonna be hearin',' Drew told him as he took the .45 out of its holster and spun the chamber.

'Put that damn thing away, this is gonna be a rifle job. Forrester don't want him walkin' away from it,' snapped Keller, angry that Drew was not taking the job as seriously as he thought Drew should be taking it.

'To hell with Forrester. S'long as the job gits done an' he pays up, what the hell?' Drew coughed, hawked and spat into the sluggish flowing river a few yards from the trail.

''Kay, this is it.' Keller hauled his horse to a halt and slid down from the saddle. Beside him, his companion dismounted and tethered the black mare to a tree, then unshipped his Winchester from the saddle boot.

Just beyond the bend, Jack Murtagh lay on his back, his hands behind his head, his eyes closed. Beside him, his homemade fishing rod rested, wedged in the mud. A sudden flurry of water brought him to his feet. Jack snatched the rod out of the mud and waded into the water a few yards, until it reached his knees. Settling his balance, Jack started to haul the line in.

Gradually, the fish lost heart and Jack pulled it to the surface. It came clear, still struggling on the end of the line.

Behind him, in a thicket, Keller and Drew raised their Winchesters. 'Easy as pissin',' Keller whispered, lining Jack up in the sights of his rifle. A second later both men fired.

The bullets struck Jack Murtagh in the spine and the base of the neck. The force pitched him forward into the clear water of the river. Within seconds his blood had started to mix with the clear river water. Keller and Drew splashed into where he lay. Catching him by the boots, they dragged him, to the bank where they dropped him face down.

'Git his horse an' a rope,' ordered Keller, placing the dead man's hands behind his back. Quickly, Drew went over to the spruce tree where Jack had tethered his horse and led it over to where Keller waited for him.

'Give me a hand gettin' him in the saddle, then we can tie him to it.' Together, they pulled the dead man up and put him over the saddle.

Keller tied his hands together while Drew secured his feet. When they had finished both men were sweating due to the heat of the day and the whiskey they had drunk.

'Glad that's over.' Drew mopped his forehead, then took his canteen from the saddle horn and drank thirstily from it.

Pulling a plug of tobacco from his vest pocket, Keller bit a lump off and started mashing it with his stained teeth.

After a while, when the flies had started gathering around Jack Murtagh's head and Milt Drew had quenched his thirst

10

sufficiently, Keller said, 'We'd best go an' break the news to Lucy Murtagh, that she's the widder Murtagh now.' His coarse laughter echoed through the valley.

The thin calico dress clung to Lucy Murtagh's slim figure as she stood in the back room of the cabin that Jack had built with the help of some neighbours on the other side of the river.

With the hem of her apron, she wiped her forehead and sighed at the heat. She did not mind Jack taking some time off to go fishing, fish that would fatten up their table. Lucy knew that he had worked hard since they had come to the valley. Mining for silver was damned hard work, but now Jack felt that a breakthrough was on the cards.

Lucy did not pretend to understand anything about mining, but Jack had made it plain to her that something big was about to break. Something that would make them rich, and get them out of the valley so they could go somewhere and buy a fine house and where she could pay someone to do her cooking and cleaning. Perhaps they could even start a family, but for now she would have to content herself with baking some bread to go with the trout that her husband intended catching for their supper.

She heard the clink of harness as a couple of horses approached the cabin from the river. Lucy frowned, she had not expected Jack to return for a couple of hours yet. She heard the cabin door open.

'Jack, is that you?' she called out. For a moment she listened. No answer. She smiled to herself, it must be his idea of a silly joke.

Going into the front room she saw Abe Keller framed in the doorway. Lucy gave a little cry of alarm as Keller peeled off his gloves and tossed them onto the table.

'Hi,' he greeted her with a smile. 'Lookin' mighty pretty today, Lucy.'

Lucy gave a shudder. Abe Keller was

one of those men who could undress a woman with a look.

'Get out, Keller,' she said nervously. 'Jack's due back any time now.'

'Jack,' he laughed. 'Jack's outside.'

For some reason this did nothing to reassure Lucy. She pushed past him and went out onto the veranda of the cabin. The first thing she saw was Milt Drew leaning against the hitching rail. Then she saw Jack's horse with Jack slung over it, his dark hair matted with blood, a big hole in the back of his vest.

'Jack. Oh Jack!' she screamed, rushing towards him.

Keller came out of the cabin onto the veranda. Before she could reach the rail, Keller caught her round the waist. Drew drank from the bottle and laughed. Keller carried Lucy into the cabin. Drew followed them in, kicking the door shut behind him.

Two

'Sorry to be losing you like this, Sergeant Guthrie,' Captain Donaldson said quietly. A troubled look ran over the Captain's face as he looked the ex-sergeant in the eye. 'Good men are hard to come by.'

'I'm sure sorry to be going this way, Captain,' Guthrie replied. Both men were standing in Captain Donaldson's office. Jed was dressed in a new set of civilian duds that he had bought with his pay-off money when they told him that his days in the Army were over. He noted with a feeling of regret that Captain Donaldson was rigged out for another campaign against the Apaches. Jed was sure sorry that he wasn't going with him like the rest of his company.

Captain Donaldson extended his hand

and grasped Jed's.

'Damn sorry about your leg. Damn sorry.' Captain Donaldson indicated Jed's left leg. An Apache bullet had smashed up the ankle, rendering him unfit for further service.

For a moment there was an awkward silence. Then Captain Donaldson broke it. 'Got any plans?'

Guthrie smiled. 'Got a couple of friends in Colorado Territory, prospecting for silver when I last heard. Jack and Lucy Murtagh. They sent me an open invitation to look them up if I got down there. Reckon I'll be getting down there sooner than I thought.'

Captain Donaldson gave a rueful smile. 'Still, it might be better than hunting Apaches.'

'Doubt it, sir,' Jed replied.

'Well, good luck.' Donaldson hesitated for a moment, then added, 'Jed.'

'Thanks Mike.' Automatically, Jed came to attention then turned and left the room.

Outside in the orderly office, Sergeant O'Brien was waiting for him and like Captain Donaldson, he grasped Jed's hand and firmly shook it, a broad grin splitting his battle-scarred Irish face.

'Thanks, Sean. And thank all the boys.' Jed turned to the door. 'An' good hunting.'

'That we'll have,' the sergeant grinned broadly. 'And we'll get Black Bear just for you.'

'You do that, Sean.' For the last time Jed Guthrie limped out of the orderly office at Fort Dillon.

He crossed the veranda to the hitch rail where he had looped the horse he had bought and that would take him part of the way to Colorado Territory.

Three

Bart Lomax, Sheriff of Bad Rock, sat in Charlie Vesty's cafe eating his breakfast. He was regretting that he had not got himself a new deputy before he had sent Sam Hutchins up to Pine Gulch to check on the next silver shipment that was coming to Bad Rock.

He watched the new arrivals moving into town. They came on foot with their bags and gear slung over their shoulders, they came on horseback, in wagons. In every way you would think of, and still they were making their way to Bad Rock.

To Bart the whole thing was a mixed blessing. There had been no denying that the economy of the town had needed a kick in the ass, but these people brought not only their hopes but also their sins, their crimes and their misdemeanours. Last night there had been a killing in the Silver Palace and a gambler would not be dealing off the bottom again or from anywhere else for that matter. Law suits over claims were piling up in the new courthouse. Bart sighed and pushed his cup away.

Through the window he saw the owner of the Silver Palace, Brad Fulsom, coming out of the batwing doors. He was tall, with a scar running down his cheek. The sort some women went for, thought Bart.

Hesitating on the boardwalk, Brad Fulsom's grey eyes searched the street. He pulled a cigar from his vest pocket and lit it. Tossing the match away, he sauntered down towards the Bad Rock Bank—a new bank that had been built in the last year to accommodate the silver bars that were sent over from the smelt for safekeeping until they were railroaded down to Denver.

For some reason, Bart watched the man. Not that he had any reason to watch him, it was just that he had a bad-ass attitude that got under Bart's skin last night when Bart had told him about some of the people who were dealing in his saloon. Fulsom had looked set to draw, but Matt Glass, his partner, just about stopped him getting himself killed. Lomax was sorry that Glass had stopped Fulsom drawing; it might save him a lot of trouble, he thought.

Fulsom headed down the street. Bart, finishing his coffee, stood up and dropped some coins on the table.

'See you, Bart,' Charlie Vesty called as he moved in on the empty table to collect the crockery and reset it for the next customer.

'Be seein' you, Charlie.' Bart raised his hand as he went into the street and headed down in the direction that Fulsom had taken.

'That nosy sheriff's headed our way,' Matt Glass said to his partner.

'Don't pay him no mind.' Fulsom knocked the ash off the end of his cigar.

'Just doing his job, that's all.'

'Might be an idea to put a bullet through that nosy head of his,' Glass replied, as he pretended to gaze into the window of a nearby shop.

'Don't be so damn stupid,' snapped Fulsom. 'We don't want any trouble until we're ready to start it.'

'Well, you're headin' this outfit. Just don't leave it too late if we have to do it.' Glass eyed his partner up and down. He didn't like the idea of working with him, but so long as it kept the folding stuff coming in he could live with it.

'The boys are up in the hills, are they?' Fulsom ground out his cigar.

'Sure, but they don't cotton to playin' miners. Reckon it ain't honest outlawin',' Glass smiled.

'You tell them from me, if they want to come out of this with any money, they'll have to put up with it,' Fulsom replied, dropping the butt of his cigar in a horse trough.

Glass shrugged. 'It's your say so. I'm gonna get some more grub for them. Ain't got much dinero, though.'

Fulsom scowled, but took the hint. Fishing out his bill fold, he handed Glass a twenty. 'Call at the back of the saloon before you go and I'll hand you a couple of bottles to keep out the cold.'

'Maybe you could run to one of them pretty ladies as well,' Glass said, grinning. 'But if you can't they'll have to make do with the whiskey. Whichever, it's mighty fine of you,' he laughed.

'You'd better believe it.' As Glass turned to go, Fulsom added. 'If this goes wrong, we could end up dancin' on air.'

'Doubt it, pard.' Glass headed towards the store.

Bart Lomax watched the exchanges from the far end of the street and would have given a lot to have heard what was said.

Bart Lomax walked thoughtfully back to his office.

Unlocking the door he went inside and

put on a fresh pot of coffee. While he was waiting for it to boil, he went to the roll-top desk and pulled out the pile of dodger posters. For nearly an hour, between cups of coffee, he studied the descriptions of the men wanted by the law. He came up with nothing. After an hour, he put the posters away and stretched his legs. As he got up the office door opened.

'Hi, Bart.' Carol Davies had the sweetest smile that Bart Lomax had ever set eyes on. Her hair hung thick and golden down to her slim shoulders and hers was the best figure in the territory. What made Bart really happy was the fact that she was his fiancée.

'Morning, Carol.' He kissed her passionately on the mouth, but she pushed him away playfully.

'It's a bit early in the day for that, besides, I've got some deliveries to make for Pa,' she laughed.

'Got anything for me?' He lifted the edge of the blue piece of linen that covered

24

the basket that Carol was carrying over her arm.

'I saw you coming out of Charlie Vesty's about an hour ago. I reckon you've had enough.' For a moment, she hesitated then said, 'If you come by the store later, I'll see what I can find for you. Where's Sam? I haven't seen him for a couple of days.'

'Sent him down to Pine Gulch see if he can get any news about when the next silver shipment's due,' Bart said with a worried look on his square face. 'Weather's been breakin' up. Sure hope he's all right.'

'There isn't a storm that could get the better of Sam Hutchins,' Carol said, picking up her basket and turning for the door.

'See you later,' Bart said.

The morning had worn on and Matt Glass had collected a gunny sack of supplies, then gone into the Silver Palace for the bottles that Fulsom had promised him for the boys up at the mine.

Stashing the bottles in his saddle bag, he headed for the peaks overlooking Bad Rock. Bart Lomax watched him go.

About the time he rode out, the train carrying freight and passengers from down the valley ground to a halt at the Bad Rock Station. Jack Burrows, the stationmaster, came along the platform collecting tickets from the few passengers who rode the train.

'Hi.' The voice startled Burrows, but the face startled him more. It was the face of a young man, but with plenty of experience in it.

'Kin I help you?' Burrows asked as he punched the stranger's ticket.

'Hope so,' the man replied. 'I'm tryin' to find some friends of mine. Name of Murtagh. Jack Murtagh. He lives hereabouts.'

'Sure. I know Jack and his missus,' Burrows brightened considerably. 'Got a place over that way.' He pointed to the peaks above Bad Rock. Quickly, he gave the stranger directions for getting to the Murtagh place.

'Much obliged.' The stranger touched the brim of his stetson and walked away.

Jed Guthrie, having got the directions to Jack Murtagh's place, went in search of a livery station. He found it at the edge of town. It had a look of being newly built and smelled of paint and pitch.

'Need any help?' a voice came from the dark above Guthrie's head.

'Need a horse for a coupla of days,' he said as he watched the youngster clamber down from the hay loft.

'Hi, I'm Nick Stannard,' the youngster said. He must have been about sixteen and had an untidy crop of black hair. He was dressed in a pair of dungarees and a grey shirt. His face was flushed and excited, something that Guthrie put down to whoever he was entertaining the loft. The boy brushed the straw off his dungarees and held out his hand.

'Jed Guthrie,' Jed returned the hand-shake.

'Got anythin' in mind?' Nick threw the long-handled rake across the aisle that held the stalls.

'As long as it's alive,' Jed smiled at the youth's good humour.

'Got a black at the bottom. Care to take a look at him?' He walked down between the stalls with Jed.

The black pawed spiritedly at the ground when Nick led him out of the stall.

'Sure 'pears to be a fine piece of horseflesh.' Jed put his warbag down on a bale of hay.

He pulled out his bill fold and peeled off a couple of bills. 'Reckon she'll suit.' He handed the bills to Nick.

'Gee, thanks. Ten's plenty,' Nick Stannard said with surprise.

'That's OK, Nick. You keep it and buy whoever's up in the loft something pretty,' Jed laughed.

The boy reddened, then glanced up at

the hay loft. 'Won't tell Pa, will you?'

With a grin, Jed shook his head. 'Not on your life,' he said as he looked round for a saddle and blanket.

'Over by the door,' Nick told him.

Jed saddled the horse and got it ready to ride.

'Keep an eye on my warbag, while I'm riding up to the Murtagh place,' he called out as Abe Keller and Milt Drew came into the alley that led to the livery.

'See you,' Nick called back.

As Jed disappeared, Keller grabbed the youth by the shirt front and slammed him against the side of the livery stable.

'That fella say he was headin' out to the Murtagh place?' Keller snarled.

Nick caught hold of his wrist and tried to shake himself loose.

Keller just laughed. 'Can't hear you.'

'He's headin' out to the Murtaghs',' Nick mumbled.

Keller and Drew exchanged glances.

'Git our horses saddled,' Keller told the youth.

'Who d'you reckon he is?' Drew leaned against the blacksmith's forge at the end of the alley.

'If he's goin' up to the Murtaghs' place it could be trouble for us. Might be better if he didn't make it.' Keller's eyes narrowed. 'You got them horses ready yet?' he called out to Nick, who had just finished saddling Keller's mount. He led him out of the livery and watched them ride after Jed.

'You comin' back up here, Nick?' The girl's voice drove everything else out of the boy's mind.

Jed had turned up the trail that led into the mountains. The going got harder and the sun stronger. Soon the sweat ran freely down his face. Taking out his bandanna he mopped it up. The mountains towered above him, the snow gleaming on their tops. Rowelling the black, Jed pushed on.

Some way behind him Keller and Drew

followed at an easy pace.

'What d'ya reckon Forrester's gonna say to this?' Drew asked his partner.

'Can't rightly say, but we'd better put a bullet in this fella, he could be anybody. If we don't put him under, he might put us under, and there's no guarantee that Forrester'd git us out. Him an' Lomax don't see eye to eye, not like he did with Sheriff Bragg.' Keller bit on a chew of tobacco then passed it to Drew.

'C'mon.' Drew pointed to a side canyon that led off the trail they had been following. Soon there was hardly enough room for them to ride side by side. An underground river flowed out from under the walls of the canyon and the horses splashed through its cold waters.

After about half an hour the trail widened as they got up onto dry ground. Another half mile on they found themselves looking at the trail that Jed would have to follow.

Keller picked a spot and he and Drew hitched their horses to a tree. The dry undergrowth snapped beneath their feet as they cut down to the trail. They waited in silence, the flies gathering round them to lick at the sweat on their faces. A sudden jangling of harness spooked the flies. Both men raised their rifles as Jed rode out of the trees.

They fired together and Jed went down.

Four

The hairs on the back of Jed's back had gone up as he passed into the undergrowth of the valley. Thick bushes were on every side. The trail became overhung with trees. In the background the black walls of the canyon reared up threateningly.

Jed slipped the leather over the hammer of his Colt, his senses alert for anything that would warn him of danger. When it came it was almost too late. The sun caught the barrel of Keller's rifle just as he squeezed the trigger.

The crack of the shot and Jed throwing himself out of the saddle happened at almost the same second. Rolling clear, he drew his Colt and waited. The wind had been driven from his body when he hit the ground. For a moment there was

33

silence. Then he heard the approach of booted steps and the sound of grass being crushed underfoot.

They came from his right. Cautiously, he raised his head. A rifle shot cut down a branch above him. Jed caught a glimpse of a figure moving in his direction. Quickly, he loosed off a shot.

'He's over there,' a voice called out. 'Can't you see him?' It was Keller, angry that the first shots had not done the job.

'No, but I got a pretty fair idea where he is,' Milt Drew replied, throwing out a shot.

Instinctively, Jed ducked but resisted the temptation to shoot back until he had a better idea of what he was shooting at. Another shot slapped into a tree beside him. One of his assailants had worked his way behind him. Another shot rang out and Jed felt a burning sensation in his arm as a bullet sliced through his flesh.

Warm, sticky blood ran down to his wrist. Behind him and to his front he could hear the undergrowth being trodden down as they closed in. Jed began to feel like a rat in a trap. The flow of blood became stronger.

'Think I can see him,' Keller called out as he caught the yellow movement of Jed's shirt against the green.

Spinning quickly, Jed suppressed a groan. Shadows flickered among the green and another shot rang out. This time it went pretty far to his right. Edging over to his right, he heard for the first time the roaring of the river somewhere below.

He strained his ears to catch any sound that might betray the presence of his attackers. He could hear nothing. By now he had moved well away from the trail, deeper into the darkness of the forest. The loss of blood made him feel light-headed, sweat pumped from his forehead. He sleeved it away and took another step to his right.

A sudden sound came out of the silence, like that of a twig snapping underfoot. Jed turned round. Some yards away he could see a figure cat-footing towards him, his rifle held across his chest. Raising the .45 Jed fired. The figure jumped back and he knew that he had missed.

Somebody snapped a shot at him. It whipped away into the trees. Backing away, Jed suddenly became conscious of the growing roar of the river sounding like a cannonade in the distance. Turning, he saw the canyon's ledge looming up only yards away.

'Kin see him,' hollered Keller, raising his rifle.

The sound of the shot was lost in the roaring of the water. The ground gave way beneath him as he plummeted into the water.

'Sure finished that son-of-a-bitch. He won't be nosin' round the Murtaghs' place now,' Keller called out as he peered over the edges of the canyon at the white foaming waters below.

There was no sign of Jed Guthrie.

Matt Glass had left Bad Rock behind him and was heading up towards the claim that he and the others had staked. It was not a real claim, just a blind where the silver bars from the Bad Rock Bank would be stashed until the heat had died down. It had been Fulsom's idea and Glass and the others thought it pretty good. Instead of making a run with a wagonload of silver that weighed the hell of a lot, why not just hide it in a silver mine, the last place anybody would think of looking?

Glass pulled off the trail and slid down from his horse as Art Kenny came out of the cabin they had thrown up. Art's face had a grin on it that told Glass things were going all right. When they had first found the place Fulsom told them that they'd need to dig out the tunnel some more. Things had got a bit quarrelsome when Kenny had handed out the shovels and picks and told the others to get digging. Kenny's fists had straightened things out and the digging had begun.

'Got some decent eats?' Kenny asked, reaching up to take the gunny sack off Glass.

'Naw, just the usual. Got a couple of bottles to keep the chill wind out, though. Courtesy of Fulsom,' laughed Glass.

Glass watched as the narrow-faced Kenny hurried back to the cabin with the food and whiskey. He knew why Kenny had been so eager to stay out in the mountains. Last summer he and two others had pulled a stick-up that had gone wrong and they had had to shoot their way out. The citizens of Pine Valley had long memories and would not rest until the men who had killed their sheriff, two women and a couple of kids going to school had trodden air or had been gunned down.

When he got in the cabin, Kenny had broken open a bottle and filled out the tin cups. Garrett lounged against the wall in greasy buckskins, his hands covered with dirt from the morning's digging. He had a thin, weaselly face with a sharp pointed chin. Blaine stood by him eyeing the cards that lay on the bunk. The clothes he stood up in had once been store-bought and had belonged to a gambler, but Blaine had caught him dealing off the bottom. Waiting for him in his hotel room he had cut the gambler's throat, taken the clothes off the body and left him his own duds, fair exchange being no robbery.

'Here,' Kenny handed him a mug. 'Any word from Fulsom about when we take this bank?'

Blaine took a slug of whiskey. 'Not yet, but it won't be too long now,' he replied, sitting himself down on a wooden box. 'How's it goin' in there?' He nodded towards the mine shaft.

Kenny shrugged. 'Uh—. We're finished. Just need some silver to fill it up with.' He laughed along with the rest of them.

Glass thought, 'Poor suckers. When that silver goes in that mine, you're goin' in with it an' stayin' there.'

'OK boys,' he said. 'Time for me to be gettin' back.'

Through the rough cut window of the cabin, Kenny, Blaine and Garrett watched him go.

'Reckon we can trust him?' Garrett finished the whiskey in his tin cup and then poured another one, his stubble-covered face all twisted up with a grin.

'Reckon y'can trust a starvin' mountain lion?' Kenny laughed.

'Just about answers it,' Blaine told them. They settled down for a night of cards.

Five

Lem Forrester was in a high old rage with Keller and Drew as they stood before him.

'You tryin' to start some kinda war?' the beefy red-faced rancher stormed at them.

'We thought we was doin' the right thing,' Keller yelled back. He had not expected this kind of reception when he had come back to the ranch to tell his boss about the nosy character who had tried to ride out to the Murtagh place.

'We'd have got away with the Murtaghs disappearing and the Lascombes when the time comes. But now you've started blasting at every saddle tramp in the territory. That damn Lomax is gonna be nosin' around. Damn it, couldn't you boys have left your shooters in their holsters for once and used your brains?'

The three men were in the parlour of the S-in-a-Circle ranch house. Keller and Drew had ridden straight back to the place to put Forrester wise.

'We figured it was the best thing to do with him askin' questions in the livery.' Keller's voice had a dry edge to it.

'In the livery?' Forrester turned on them. He narrowed his eyes. 'Anybody else in there?' He thrust his reddening face in front of Keller's.

For a moment Keller said nothing.

'Yeah, that two-bit kid that looks after the place. Was him that told us. Think his pa owns the place.' His mouth went dry as he spoke. Any time now, he thought, we're gonna be off the payroll. An' workin' for the S-in-a-Circle is the best thing we've had for many day.

'Jesus H Christ,' Forrester breathed, his rage steadily working up. 'Find out what the kid knows and then ....' he hesitated.

'Fix him,' Keller finished the sentence for him.

Forrester stalked over to him, his rage barely under control. 'Yeah, fix him.'

'Right, boss,' Keller said, backing out of the parlour.

Isabel Forrester slipped quietly up the stairs to her room when she heard Keller and Drew start towards the door.

Quietly, she closed her bedroom door and waited until she heard them leave. It had shaken her a mite to hear Keller and Drew saying that they had killed the Murtaghs, for that was the only inference she could draw from what had been said in the parlour, knowing that her pa had hired them to do his dirty work. Not that she minded that. Lem Forrester had fought for this land, even to the extent of sacrificing his wife. Isabel knew he would not let anybody take it off him. That was not the reason for her dislike of the two who had left the house. There was just something about them, especially Keller.

43

He frightened her. The other, Milt Drew, wasn't too bad, but she still did not like him. Going to the window she watched both men going to the bunkhouse.

Jed had smashed the surface of the river and straightaway lost consciousness. His body floated, half-submerged, through the white, swirling waters, crashing against the rocks and branches before finally snagging against the bank.

Slowly, he came to just as Jilly Lascombe, the daughter of a silver miner, came down to the water's edge to wash some clothes. 'Hey, pa,' she called out as she caught hold of Jed's sleeve as the water started to pull him along. Anxiously, she turned her head. Downstream the river started to speed up as it roared over the falls to the rocks below.

Barry Lascombe heard his daughter's call and dropped the pick that he was carrying.

'What is it?' he yelled, wiping his hands

on the front of his trousers and running towards the river's edge.

'Give me a hand, Pa. This fella's slipping away from me.'

Seeing Jilly holding onto the man's sleeve, Barry rushed down to her and helped her drag Jed to the side.

'Let's see what you've caught there,' he said to Jilly as he laid Jed on his back.

'Nasty-looking wound,' he said, fingering the hole in Jed's arm. 'Reckon he'll weather it, though. Come on, let's git him somewhere dry.' He did not need his daughter's help to carry Jed up to the cabin and put him on the bunk.

'Find some of my old clothes and something to dry him off with. An' there's a bottle of whiskey in the old box under my bunk.'

'Oh,' Jilly laughed, 'that's where you keep it, is it?'

But her father had already started to pull off Jed's clothes. When his daughter came back Barry dried Jed off and cleaned the wound by pouring the whiskey into it.

'There, that'll hold the wound,' he said as he bandaged it up.

'Wonder who he is?' mused Jilly as she wiped his face.

Barry smiled. 'He can tell you himself when he comes round. That's if you can wait that long.'

As soon as darkness had fallen Isabel went to the stable and saddled up her horse. It had been two days since she had seen anything of Brad Fulsom, but this morning he had left a note for her to meet him in the old abandoned cabin that they used for their lovemaking.

When he had first come to Bad Rock he had opened up the saloon and invited her father and several prominent local citizens to a small get-together, Her father, in turn, had invited Fulsom to the ranch. And that was where they met. Having led a sheltered life since the death of her mother, Isabel found herself immediately taken by his dashing good looks. The scar on his face made him even more appealing.

Had he known of her relationship with Fulsom her father would have put a stop to it, but being so taken up with the running of the ranch he did not have the time to keep his daughter on as tight a rein as he should have done.

Consequently, Isabel managed to slip away from the ranch and see Fulsom whenever he left the note in the tree for her.

To Fulsom, the liaison with Isabel was no more than a passing fancy, something to amuse him in Bad Rock while he waited until the time was ripe for them to relieve the bank of its hoard of silver. The sooner the job was done, the sooner he could forget about Isabel Forrester, no matter how desirable he found her.

A light flared among the trees as Isabel reached the rendezvous. Eagerly she climbed down from the horse and rushed to the cabin. Inside, she flung her arms around Brad Fulsom. Fulsom smiled as he put his arms round her narrow waist. This was the one sight of Bad Rock he would sure as hell miss.

Several hours later Bart Lomax had just started his rounds and was standing under the veranda of his office when he saw the horse and rider making their way slowly into town. He stood back a-ways so that the late rider would not see him. His eyebrows went up as he recognized the rider as Brad Fulsom. Fulsom guided his horse down the alley to the back of the quiet and shuttered Silver Palace.

Fulsom's behaviour intrigued the sheriff. Why hadn't Fulsom been dealing in the Silver Palace? And where the hell had he been? There was nothing to prevent a man riding quietly back into town. After dark. Bearing the incident in mind, Bart continued on his rounds.

The sheriff walked along the block, checking the doors of the shops, then across to the general store, round past the shacks that were springing up on the edge of town and finally round the small town of tents that the miners had thrown up. A shiver ran through his body as he turned back towards his office and a mug of coffee. Suddenly, his senses stirred as his ears picked out the sound of a second horse approaching town.

Lomax watched from the shadows with some surprise as the rider turned out to be Matt Glass. Now that was odd he thought to himself. Glass went the same way as Fulsom had done, down the alley and into the saloon.

For a moment he hesitated, then Bart moved towards the alley, knowing that what he was about to do was not strictly legal. He crouched down beside the pile of empty beer casks and listened at a partly open window.

The voices of Fulsom and Glass were indistinct and he could only make out the occasional word. Glass was doing all the talking. Suddenly, all hell broke loose behind Bart and the talking inside stopped.

Turning quickly, his hand on his gun, Bart made out the figure of a drunk lurching about in the alley among the overturned beer casks. He almost laughed when he recognized Al Fryer, the town drunk, struggling to keep on his feet among the casks.

Thinking quickly, he ran towards Fryer and catching him by the shoulder propelled him out of the alley and into the street. A look over his shoulder told him that the rear door of the saloon had been opened and he could just make out the figure of Fulsom in the light cast from the office.

'What's going on?' Fulsom yelled into the street.

'Just a drunk looking for some more beer,' Bart called back.

Fulsom came running to the top of the alley, gun in hand. 'Oh, it's you, Sheriff,' he called in surprise.

'Just gonna take him down to jail so he can sleep it off. Ain't that so, Al?' Bart stifled any protests that Al might have made.

Six

Matt Glass had remained in the saloon's office when Fulsom had gone outside to see what was causing the ruckus. Hearing the exchange between Fulsom and the sheriff, he suspected that it had been Lomax outside all the time. Once or twice he had noticed the sheriff watching him and Fulsom and wondered if he was cottoning on to anything.

'Think we should be reconsidering doing something about that sheriff,' he said to Fulsom when they had returned to the office. Fulsom reached out for the bottle and filled up the glass he had been drinking from, the heat from Isabel's passion having long ago subsided.

Behind Fulsom the door opened and the barman came in.

'He gone?' Fulsom asked.

'Yeah, boss,' the barman told him.

'Night, Mac,' Fulsom said as the barman went out.

Bart Lomax had locked Al Fryer up in the jail and was brewing some fresh coffee for himself with Al's thick snoring to keep him company. Nursing the coffee he heard the sharp tap of a woman's boots on the boardwalk outside. With a grin he got to his feet. Pulling back the peephole, he smiled when he saw Carol outside.

'What are you doin' out at this time of night?' Bart asked severely when he had let her into the office.

'Ma said you hadn't been round for any supper, so I brought you some over.' She pointed to the basket she had put on the desk, then kissed him passionately. Bart put his arms round her neck and held her tightly. They kissed, only stopping long enough to come up for air.

'It's going cold,' Carol said breathlessly

as she straightened her hair.

'Guess so,' Bart pulled back the cover. The basket contained a heap of freshly roasted chicken, fresh bread and apple pie. It looked and smelled better than Charlie Vesty's cooking. Bart grinned at the thought. Good job he was marrying Carol and not Charlie Vesty or he would be going hungry on a regular basis.

'Coffee?' he asked, raising the pot.

'You make it?' Carol enquired, raising her eyebrows.

'Sure I made it. There's nothing wrong with it,' Bart grimaced.

'I'll wait until I get home,' Carol told him with a laugh.

'OK, it's your loss,' Bart replied with a chuckle.

'I doubt it,' she said, reaching for the door handle. 'Just don't drink too much. Looks as if it could be bad for your insides,' she said.

Lomax got up and kissed her. He walked her down to the store that her parents owned. Only when he had seen the lamp come on in her room did Bart Lomax return to the office and the food that Carol had brought.

Keller and Drew had watched Matt Glass ride out of town and up the trail. They gave him plenty of time to get clear, then edged their horses onto the trail.

'Wonder where he's goin'?' Drew hissed as he passed them.

'Dunno, an' I don't rightly care,' Keller replied in an irritated tone. 'You kin bet it ain't none of our business.'

The living quarters for the Bad Rock livery stable were above the stable itself. Nick mainly used them. His ma and pa had a little house in the middle of town. Nick usually stayed overnight if it looked like getting busy and tomorrow was Saturday, the day most miners usually took off to get some liquor and play some cards; and when they did it stretched into the Sabbath.

Nick had been asleep for some time when Keller and Drew left their horses round the back of the livery.

'Best git up on the roof and find a handy window,' Keller whispered as he and his companion sneaked around the sides of the building. 'Otherwise we're gonna be wakin' the horses inside.'

Both men turned their heads upwards to the roof of the lean-to they had found. 'There it is.' Keller reached for the drainpipe, then hauled himself up, with Drew coming behind him. They went hand over hand until they reached the roof.

Keller swung himself up as quietly as he could and cat-footed along the roof until he reached the window.

Pushing against the window pane, he found the lock was firmly on. He thrust the blade of his knife up against the catch and levered it until it gave. Then he slid the window up. The light of the moon gave on to the bed up against the wall.

Swiftly Keller made certain that there

was nothing he could fall over, then stepped inside.

Both men's eyes had adjusted to the darkness. Keller pointed to the lamp on the table. Drew understood immediately. He pulled out a match and struck it on the heel of his boot.

The boy opened his eyes slowly, and tried to raise his hand to shield them from the light.

Keller grabbed the wrist and held it tightly.

'This is a gun pointing at your head,' he told Nick, 'so keep quiet and do as you're told.'

'OK, mister,' Nick said shakily.

'That hombre that passed through and asked about the Murtagh place. Who was he an' what did he want?' Keller asked viciously, pressing the gun against Nick's temple.

'Name's Guthrie, Jed Guthrie. Didn't say what he wanted up there.' Nick's voice trembled.

Pressing the gun harder against the boy's temple Keller snarled, 'Yer lyin'.'

'Honest, I ain't.' Nick tried to twist away from the barrel of the pistol which had started to draw blood.

'Sounds like he's tellin' the truth,' Drew told Keller.

'Then we had a wasted ride.' Keller's voice told Drew what he had in mind. Like a striking snake, Keller snatched the pillow from under Nick's head and pushed it over his face before firing into it. The bed shook once under the muffled gunshot.

'Let's git before somebody comes looking for his horse.'

Keller thrust the .45 into its holster and went for the window. He stopped, seeming to have second thoughts. Hurrying back to the bed, he picked up the lamp and smashed it against the wall.

In seconds the flames had started licking at the dry wood, but by then the killers were climbing down the drainpipe to the ground.

No one had heard the shot because it was muffled by the pillow, but the horses in the stalls, sensing that something was wrong, started kicking and pulling at the ropes that held them as the fire took hold.

When he finished eating, Bart Lomax checked that Al Fryer still snored in his cell. Outside, the Colorado air felt good in his lungs. Bart yawned and stretched. From the corner of his eye he caught the reddening glow in the sky from the direction of the livery stable.

'Hell and damnation,' he called out, racing towards the livery. Bart pulled his gun from its holster and fired two quick shots into the air. The two shots were the fastest way he could think of to raise the alarm. His first thought was to get down to the livery and rouse Nick so that they could get the horses out.

When he got down there, Bart shot the lock off the door and went inside. The livery had filled with smoke. The tied-up horses were panicking and kicking wildly at the sides of their stalls as the smoke started to thicken.

Bart hauled out his knife and slashed the ropes holding the terrified animals, at the same time calling out for Nick. The wooden steps leading to the living quarters were situated at the back of the livery. By the time Bart had worked his way down there they were ablaze, and rafters were falling from the upper storey.

When he reached the wooden steps leading to where Nick slept, Bart could see that it was impossible to go further. A great blanket of smoke was drifting down towards him, flames were eating at the stairs, but there was a sudden crash above him as the top of the stairs came hurtling down, narrowly missing him.

Bart staggered back, barely avoiding the falling wood. He decided that the time had come to get out. Staggering back down the aisle of flames, he reached the door of the stable as the ceiling came down.

Tugging off the bandanna, Bart gulped in great lungfuls of night air. The air soon revived him and as it did he became aware of running feet and the sound of wheels as the fire team hauled the engine round the corner. A rough hand fell on Bart's shoulder and pushed him away.

'Done all you can, Bart, firing off those shots. It's our chore now.' He turned to see Bill Griffiths, captain of the fire team, standing beside him and shouting orders to his men as they got the hoses hooked up and tried to put the fire out.

Leaving the fire team to its task, Bart got out of the way and stood by the corner.

'Bart, Bart.' He felt the arms round his chest and sensed Carol's soft face pressing against his. 'Are you all right?'

'Yeah, honey,' he said, pressing her close to him.

'What about young Nick?' she asked anxiously, looking over at the burning livery.

'Unless he got out before I got there, I

don't think he made it. Nick wouldn't have left them horses in there.' Bart watched as the colour drained from her face. He felt her shake as he put his hands on her shoulders.

For a moment he thought she was going to pass out. He held on to her tightly.

'Come on. I'll get you back home and make sure your ma an' pa put you to bed.' He guided her along the street away from the burning building and the crowd that had started to gather.

Carol's ma and pa were waiting for them at the front door of the general store. They gave him a smile and took Carol into the store.

'Comin' in fer some coffee or a glass of whiskey? Guess there's a bottle in the kitchen someplace.' Les Davies led Bart through the store into the back living room.

Bart flopped down in a chair and dropped his stetson on the floor beside him. As he did so, the realization that sooner or later he would have to face Nick's parents came to him. He shuddered at what they must feel like at having lost an only child.

Upstairs he could hear the two women moving about. Les came back with two glasses. He handed one to Bart. Neither man had much to say after Bart had told Les that he believed that Nick had not got out of the livery. He finished up his drink and stood up.

'Gonna have to break it to Nick's folks,' he said to the shaken-looking Les.

'That's one chore I sure don't envy you.' Les had seen him to the door.

Almost everybody in town was on Main Street and that included a lot of the miners. Bart walked back towards the home of Nick's parents. As he got to the house, the door opened and Nick's ma came out onto the veranda. Her face had a pale haggard look to it.

'Nick was in there, wasn't he?' Sarah Stannard said.

'I ain't rightly sure,' Bart's voice faltered as he spoke.

'You know he was, where else would he be?' the woman persisted.

'Guess he was. Ain't anything I can say.' Bart had removed his hat and was holding it, his fingers twisting and untwisting the brim.

'Guess you'd better go, Bart. We've got some grieving to do.' Bart turned to walk down the path, but then she called out to him, 'Thanks for coming round.' A second later he heard the door close.

As he trudged back to his office and the early morning light started to come up, Bart could see that there was no possibility of the fire from the livery spreading to the rest of the town.

He threw his stetson on the rack and flopped down in his chair. Sitting down Bart started to worry about how the fire might have got started. Nick had had a wild streak in him and was making a name for himself as a beau with the local girls, but however Bart looked at it, he could not see Nick doing anything that would endanger either the town, the livery or the horses under his care.

Seven

'Ready for some food?' Jilly Lascombe smiled at Jed as he struggled to sit up in the bed.

'And then some,' he grinned as the girl pulled the pillow up behind him and straightened the bedclothes out in front of him.

'Fine, it won't take long. Pa's just had his and gone up to the mine,' she said.

Jed yawned. He felt the hell of a lot better than he had done when he hit the water with a bullet in him. Barry Lascombe had dug it out with a sharp Bowie knife and cauterized the wound with flame and whiskey. After thrashing about in some pain for a spell, he had dropped into an easy sleep.

The smell of Jilly cooking breakfast for

her pa brought him out of it with a runny mouth.

The door opened and Jilly backed in holding a tray with a plateful of ham and eggs. Beside the ham and eggs stood a mug of coffee. Laying the plate out, she stood back while Jed laid into the food with a will. Soon the plate was empty of food and the mug drained of coffee.

'Want some more?' Jilly asked.

'Heck no. Wouldn't mind some more of this coffee though.' He held the mug towards her.

Giving him a warm smile, Jilly went back to the kitchen, where she refilled the mug.

'How come somebody decided to use you for target practice, if it isn't a personal question?' she asked, handing him the mug.

'Ain't a personal question at all. Thought somebody was after the few dollars I got in my bill fold, but now I think they were after my hide.'

'Who'd you upset?' She brushed aside the long hank of black hair. 'Some big timer from round hereabouts?'

'Don't know anybody from hereabouts, big or small.' The ex-sergeant scratched his chin thoughtfully.

'Well,' Jilly continued, 'might have something to do with the trouble we've been having. Only I can't see how.'

'Same kinda trouble I teamed up with yesterday?' he asked.

'Somebody's been taking pot shots at me and Pa. Haven't caught anybody at it, but it doesn't take a big brain to tie a name to him.'

'An' just who would this be that you don't have to have a big brain to tie a name to?' he asked.

'Lem Forrester, that's who.' Jilly took a step closer to the bed.

'He the local bad man?' Jed asked, beginning to feel a little embarrassed by the way that Jilly was looking at him.

'No. He owns a lot of territory in these

parts. Started pestering Pa to sell up when he found out that Pa was getting close to striking silver.' Jilly sat on the edge of the bed.

Jed told her, 'I was goin' up to see Jack and Lucy Murtagh. They far from you?'

'Their place and ours are joined up. Jack seemed all excited when I saw him in town last Monday morning. Been into Bad Rock to pick up supplies. Haven't seen either Jack or Lucy since.'

Jed's black brows furrowed. He did not like what he was hearing. He had not been in Bad Rock long enough to spit. The only place he had been was the livery stable to pick up a horse and on the way up there somebody had started throwing lead at him.

He locked his fingers and put his hands behind his head. The sooner he was up there the better. 'What about the law? It been any help?'

'The law's Bart Lomax an' he says

we haven't got anything on Forrester,' Jilly said.

'Way I feel reckon it's time I went up and saw that Jack and Lucy were OK. Then pay my respects to the sheriff, if it ain't.'

Pulling back the sheets, he suddenly realized that the only thing he had on was his skin. 'My clothes fit to wear?' he asked.

'Oh, yeah, they're out back drying off on the line I rigged up. Pa cleaned your gun up as well.' She went out to get the clothes.

He got up and held the sheet round his body. A few minutes later he heard a knock on the door, and Jilly came in with his clothes over her arm, his gunbelt looped over her shoulder.

She went out while the wounded man dressed himself with only a little stiffness in his arm. He fastened on his gunbelt then drew the gun and checked it. Barry had done a good job of cleaning it up. He

71

dropped it back into the holster and went into the kitchen where Jilly was drying the breakfast dishes.

'Pa says you can take the mare out back. You can just leave it at the livery in town,' Jilly said as she dried her hands. 'He's just up the trail if you want to say goodbye.'

'I'll do that. Might call in after I've been up to see Jack and Lucy.' Jed went out to the rear of the cabin where he found the mare ready for him. He swung up into the saddle and headed up the trail.

'Goin' up to see Jack and Lucy,' Jed called out from the saddle when he saw Barry by the stream cleaning his tools.

'If I can do anything for them, let me know on your way back,' he said as he waved Jed on.

Rowelling the horse, Jed headed up towards the cabin.

When he got up there he had to admit that Jack and Lucy had picked a fine spot to build on. He pushed the horse on, sensing as he approached that something was wrong. No smoke rose from the chimney, the cabin door swung open and closed on the light breeze.

Dismounting, Jed drew his gun and cocked it.

'Jack, Lucy. You in there?' he called out.

He tried once more, his hand resting on the hitch rail. Still no answer. Tentatively, he mounted the steps. The boards under his booted feet creaked. He called out once more then kicked the door open and went inside.

The room seemed cold, despite the sun shining strongly outside. On the other side of the room a door stood open. From what Jed could see, it was the bedroom. Going inside, he found the bedclothes pulled this way and that. Something on the pillow caught his eye. He bent over and ran his fingers over it. Dried blood. Suddenly he knew what had happened to Jack and Lucy.

Swearing angrily, Jed went outside. He

waited beneath the veranda, his eyes looking for anything that might give him some idea of where the couple might be.

Going to his horse, he noticed a mess of tracks leading up to the hitch rail. Evidently someone had visited the place. He looked round until he saw the horses moving away. And from the look of things and what he could see with his limited tracking skills, the third horse was carrying a heavier burden when it moved away than when it approached the cabin.

The tracks did not lead far, just to the entrance of the mine shaft. The horses had stopped or had been stopped, the bootmarks told him that someone had gone into the mine entrance. Slowly, still unsure as to what he might find, Jed entered the mine. The dark and cold engulfed him so that he shivered, but he felt better when he found a candle pushed into a wire holder on the wall.

Lighting it, he moved forward, the cold in the mine getting more and more intense.

The light from the candle wavered and flickered. Cupping it, Jed stopped and held out the candle. Its weak light fell on something against the mine wall. At first, Jed thought the heap might be old clothes.

Bending down he held the candle up close to the dead faces of the people he had travelled far to see. The faces were white and he could see that Lucy had been shot in the temple. There were two bullet holes in Jack.

At the entrance to the shaft Jed found a shovel and dug two graves. After he had fashioned the crosses, he said a few words and rode back to town.

Eight

'Lookin' for somethin' fella?' The man tapped Jed on the shoulder as he stood outside the smouldering ruins of the livery stable.

'Sure. I was lookin' for the livery stable,' he said as he tilted back his stetson. 'Or the sheriff's office.'

'If I wuz you, I'd make it the sheriff's office. Jus' turn left an' keep walkin'. It's at the end of Main Street.' The man turned and walked off.

Following the instructions, Jed soon found himself outside the office of Bart Lomax. Hitching his horse to the rail, he went inside.

Bart Lomax was writing a report on the fire at the livery stable for the town council.

'What can I do for you?' the lawman asked, swivelling the chair round to face Jed.

'You the law round here?' Jed asked.

'This says I am,' Lomax fingered the tin on his chest.

'I've been up to see Jack and Lucy Murtagh. Somebody's shot 'em.' Jed spoke quietly, but his quietness could not conceal his anger.

'Damn,' Lomax exploded. 'Any idea what happened?'

'Reckoned that's why they pay you,' Jed told him.

'Sure, that's why they pay me. But I thought you might give me a head start. And come to that, who are you?'

'Jed Guthrie. I noticed the new telegraph office. If you want to you can wire the War Department in Washington. They'll tell you who I am and where I was discharged.'

'I'll do that.' Lomax pulled a piece of paper across the desk while Jed gave him his details.

'If you've been up there maybe there's something you can tell me.' Lomax was becoming more and more irritated with Jed's attitude.

'Could say I was an acquaintance of Jack and Lucy's. There's just some tracks leading to the mine shaft where the bodies were thrown. I buried them decent while I was up there.' Jed took the mug of coffee that Lomax had poured.

'OK, I'll go up there,' Lomax said.

'Somethin' else besides. On the trail up to Jack's place, somebody threw a heap of lead my way.' He pointed to his shoulder.

'How'd you get fixed up?' Lomax finished his coffee and dropped the mug in a pail of water.

Jed told him about the Lascombes. 'And Jilly told me that they're having some sort of trouble with a local hombre called Lem Forrester. Maybe that's where you should start looking.'

'They've been telling me that too, but

it just don't figure. Forrester's a bit of a rough hand, but I don't figure him stooping to this kinda thing. It don't set right. Lem's got too much to lose.'

'In my experience they're just the fellas that do. The more they get the more they want,' Jed told the sheriff.

'I'll get up there as soon as I can. We had a fire here last night, probably saw what was left of our livery stable on yer way into town. Young fella by the name of Nick died in it. Gotta find out how that got started, but it was probably an accident,' Lomax said, rubbing his tired-looking eyes.

'Nick?' Guthrie asked in surprise.

'Yeah. You know him as well?' Lomax asked in exasperation.

'No, just met him yesterday when I went to hire a horse.' Bad Rock was sure an eventful town, Jed thought.

'You sure you ain't got anything that can help me with that?' Lomax asked as the exertions in the livery suddenly started to make themselves felt.

The appearance of Carol stopped the argument from going further.

'Can practically smell the gunsmoke in here,' Carol said as she approached them.

Both men looked at her.

'Guess I'll be goin',' Jed told Lomax finally and went out into the street.

'Who is that handsome devil?' Carol asked as she started to unpack the basket with some food in it for Lomax.

Lomax told Carol about Jed and who he was.

'Oh, I haven't seen either of them for a couple of days,' Carol said with a smile.

'Don't reckon on seein' them again,' Bart told her.

'Why? Have they moved out?' Carol's tone was one of puzzlement.

He said quickly, 'No, they're dead. That's why Guthrie came in. Found their bodies in the mine shaft.'

Carol's face paled as she heard the news.

She had known the Murtaghs reasonably well, but that and the knowledge that Nick Stannard had died in the fire stunned her.

'Just an unfortunate accident,' Lomax told her, steadying her by holding her arms.

'Still,' Carol said, recovering herself, 'it's no consolation to his parents. I think I'd better go and see them.' She pulled the loop of the basket over her arm and lightly kissed her fiancé on the cheek.

The door of the office opened.

'Morning, Carol. Morning Bart.' Doctor Thaddius Medgrave, Bad Rock's physician, tipped his hat as he came in.

'Hi, Doc.' Bart stood aside to allow him to come in as Carol left.

'Your young lady seems a mite upset this morning. Wouldn't have anything to do with what happened last night, would it?' The doctor pulled out the cigar case he carried and offered it to Lomax, who shook his head. The match flared as he struck it and applied it to the cigar.

'Yeah, last night was pretty bad,' Lomax said with a tone of resignation in his voice.

Doc Medgrave blew the smoke towards the window. 'Worse than you think,' he said deliberately.

'Oh hell,' muttered the sheriff.

The doctor took out his linen handkerchief and opened it out so that the piece of metal it contained fell out on to the desk.

'Where'd you get that?' Lomax asked, recognizing the misshapen bullet.

'Out of Nick Stannard's body,' the doctor said, knocking the ash off his cigar.

'It is worse than I think.' Lomax sat down on the edge of his desk.

'And we both know that Nick didn't have that kind of enemy,' the doc said, regarding the end of his cigar.

'Not a one. Somethin' else, too,' Lomax said, wondering where he could find an easier job.

'What's that?' Doc Medgrave sprawled back in the chair, his long legs taking up the space between him and Bart.

'Fella just came in. Told me the Murtaghs had been shot.' Lomax's voice had become weary.

'Who the hell'd want to do that to two decent folks like them?' Medgrave gasped, the ash falling off the end of his cigar.

'Dunno, but it seems like the Lascombes are having more trouble. The fella that's just been in took a bullet while he was up there,' the sheriff said.

'If it's the fella I saw headin' up to Charlie Vesty's, he looks like trouble. Thought finding silver up here would be a blessing. Now I ain't so sure.' Doc Medgrave got up. 'Anyway, I got a few calls to make.'

'Thanks, Doc,' Lomax said as he stood up and took the paper with Jed Guthrie's details on it. 'I'll walk down with you. I've got a telegram to send.'

Nine

The ride down to Bad Rock had given Jed an appetite. He had seen the signs for Charlie Vesty's place and decided to give it a try before heading back to Jilly's.

He rode up to the Lascombe place and watched Jilly come out of the cabin as he climbed out of the saddle. It struck him then, for the first time, just what a good-looking woman she was.

'Hi, stranger,' she laughed. 'What brings you back here?'

'Thought you might need some help.' Jed tethered the horse to the hitch rail.

Jilly's face fell a little as he reminded her of her and her pa's trouble.

Walking over to her, he put his hands round her shoulders. It seemed the most natural thing in the world.

'Can't see Pa having any objections,' she told him as she looked up into his eyes.

'Neither can I,' said a voice behind them.

Jed immediately pulled himself free from Jilly, dropped to one knee and spun round, his gun in his hand.

'Mighty smart piece of work,' Barry said admiringly.

'Seems I'm going to need it if you decide to let me stick around,' Jed replied.

'Sure and we could use the help,' Barry Lascombe replied.

'Yeah, I figure I owe you for what you did,' Jed told him with a slow smile.

'Let's chew on it while we eat,' Barry said, heading for the cabin.

Jed followed them in and sat down while Jilly made some coffee for them. After a few minutes she came back into the room and set the mugs down before them. They drank in silence for a few moments, then Barry broke the silence.

'Got to warn you if you're gonna stay and

help us, then it's liable to be dangerous.'

Jed smiled as he blew the steam from the coffee.

'Yeah, I kinda figured that out for myself.'

As he spoke he noticed the half-hopeful, half-worried expression on Jilly's face.

Barry smiled to himself.

'OK, Pa,' Jilly said as she rose from the table. 'I'll fix something to eat, you fix a bed for our visitor.'

'That's fine by me,' Barry said as he looked around the room. 'But it looks as though you're gonna be sleepin' in here.'

'Suits me, but I don't figure on sleepin' much, least of all in here,' Jed said slowly. 'I'll be outside most of the time, in case these jaspers figure on shootin' us out of our beds.'

Jilly disappeared into the kitchen while Barry hauled out some blankets for Jed to sleep on. The men had decided to take it in turns in patrolling the outside of the cabin during the night.

Eventually, Jilly brought in the food. 'You're gonna need it, it gets kind of cold up here during the night,' she told them.

They ate in silence. When the meal was done night had started to fall over the valley and the shadows of the mountains fell across the cabin.

'I'll take the first shift,' Barry said to Jed as he checked the loads in his gun.

'That's fine by me,' replied Jed, finishing off his coffee.

'Be seein' you then.' Barry pulled on his hat and went outside into the gathering gloom.

'More coffee?' Jilly asked when she came back into the room.

'Reckon not,' Jed told her with a smile. 'Best be getting some sleep.'

'Be seeing you then.' Jilly lit the lamp and went into her room.

Spreading out the blanket, Jed got down on the floor in front of the dying embers of the fire.

It did not take him long to fall into an untroubled sleep.

A rough shaking woke him.

'OK Jed. It's all quiet out there.' Barry struck a match to light the lamp with. The light made Jed blink as he got up.

The wind bit through his jacket as he crossed the yard to the corral. Jed intended to make it his vantage point. He took a look back to the cabin, then started to prowl his territory. The time crawled by. He had covered the area three times before he heard the first soft footfall somewhere among the trees.

Hauling out his .45 Jed pulled back the hammer. Using the post of the corral as cover he moved down to where the sound had come from. At first he could see nothing, then a shape moved out from the trees and towards the cabin.

Jed raised his gun, then hesitated. In the hands of the approaching figure a light flared. It puzzled Jed, then he realized what it was: dynamite. He fired twice, as the figure drew back his arm to throw the stick.

There was a scream. Jed threw himself backwards as the lighted stick of dynamite fell to the ground. A bright light momentarily illuminated the yard, the earth shook with the explosion. Jed felt himself pulled clear of the earth by a giant hand then dropped unceremoniously back, the wind driven from his body. Soil and stones showered his breathless body. Shakily, Jed got to his feet, aware of the cabin door opened and Barry calling out into the night.

'I got him, Barry, but there may be more of them,' Jed gasped, pulling back the hammer of the gun.

A sound behind him made him turn. It was Barry who had crossed from the cabin to join him.

'Think I caught sight of a couple of them on the edge of the clearing,' Barry told him, and as he spoke a fusillade of shots rang out through the night, spanging away as they struck the fence of the corral.

'Seems as though you were right,' Jed grinned, despite the situation.

'Those flashes were just over there off to the right. Let's go see if we can flush them,' Jed spoke quietly.

'You go to the left, I'll go to the right,' Barry said as he moved silently away into the darkness.

Jed moved out after him, his gun held out in front of him. The area had become silent now that the sudden noise from the dynamite had subsided along with the shooting.

It took Jed only a few seconds to make the cover of the trees. Then he heard the whinnying of horses near by. He cat-footed through the trees down to the trail where the two horses had been hitched. A sudden movement between the horses made him freeze. It was the second man.

'Hold it,' Jed called out.

Without waiting the shadowy assailant

turned and threw a shot at Jed. Jed fired at the gunflash. A second later, he heard a cry of pain and the crashing of a body as it hit the ground.

'You got them?' Jilly asked when the two men returned to the cabin.

'Jed got them both,' Barry said, filling out three mugs of coffee.

'Thanks.' Jed took the mug and swallowed from it.

'We've left the one that Jed shot outside. Guess I'll take a look at him when it gets a mite lighter, see if we can figure out who he is.'

Jed drained his mug and put it on the table. 'Got a shovel and a gunny sack?' he asked of Barry.

'Sure, there's a shovel just by the door. Gunny sack's sitting on the table in the back.'

'I'll get it,' Jilly said, hurrying into the back room.

Jed took the sack from her and went outside.

'What do you reckon he wants them for?'

Jilly shook her head and shrugged.

Outside Jed picked up the shovel and went down to where the remains of the man with the dynamite were scattered.

Ten

From across the street Brad Fulsom had watched Carol enter the sheriff's office. As he climbed into the saddle a thought struck him. When the silver came up from Pine Gulch an escort of gunmen rode with it. They were half a dozen professional guns headed by Seth Wolfram. They would ride shotgun up the valley with it and bed down in the bank overnight.

Fulsom had worked out a plan to hide the silver once they got it. But the hard part of the plan had been getting the silver. Seth Wolfram's men were a pretty hard riding bunch, who didn't waste their time on prisoners. If Fulsom's men tangled with them, not only would they not get the silver they'd be shot to bits as well. Seeing the sheriff's girlfriend taking a basket to the office put the idea into his head. When Wolfram's boys spent the night in the bank, Carol always took hot grub over for them. And Carol had a set of parents to worry about. It was a cinch, he told himself, getting into the saddle and galloping out to see Isabel.

His mood was still good when he got up to the cabin and laid the fire. Fulsom had stashed a couple of buffalo robes in the cupboard. He stretched one out on the floor. Then he poured himself a drink from the bottle of brandy he also kept in the cupboard along with a pair of glasses. Isabel liked a drink before they got started. Brad Fulsom had a quick drink, then went to the window as Isabel dismounted and led the mare around to the rear of the cabin where she left it tethered in the lean-to.

'Hi, hon,' he said, catching her round the waist and whirling her off her feet.

He kissed her full and hard on the mouth, just the way she liked it.

When he had let go of her, she quickly untied the cloak from around her shoulders and let it fall to her feet. Slipping off his jacket, Fulsom tossed it across the old chair before he poured a couple of drinks. Soon they were both buck naked and sprawled on the buffalo robe.

Their lovemaking was frenzied and energetic. Fulsom had tried a couple of times to get her to slow down and take it easy so they could enjoy it more, but Isabel could not or would not. She just threw herself into it. When they had finished, their bodies were damp with sweat. Isabel's hair had matted itself against her forehead.

'Drink, honey?' Fulsom sweet-talked her, holding the glass and the bottle up to her.

'Thanks.' Her green eyes watched as the brandy spilled into the glass. They sipped it together.

When they had finished the drink, Isabel said, 'Brad.'

The muscles in Fulsom's belly knotted up, like the way they had knotted up when a drunken cowboy had caught him dealing off the bottom of the pack in a Deadwood saloon. With a woman it could only mean one thing.

'I love you, Brad.' Sensuously she ran her fingers through the thick, black hair that trailed across his chest.

'Love you too, Isabel.' He tried to sidetrack her by teasing her nipples.

She pulled away and sat up. 'We've got to think about the future, Brad.'

'Sure, honey. Just don't think that now's a good time,' Fulsom temporized.

'Oh, Brad,' she said coaxingly, kissing him lightly on the cheek. 'You do love me, don't you?'

'Would I be up here with you, if I didn't love you?' He stroked her hair.

'Guess not, honey. But we've got the future to think about. You don't want to be a rolling stone all your life? Playing cards and the like. Don't you think the time's come to put down a few roots and raise a family?' she asked, looking up at him.

Fulsom's mouth was dry. 'Well,' he temporized again. This he hadn't counted on. 'Suppose it's getting that way.' One thing would get him out of this conversation. He kissed her on the mouth and pulled her to him.

'Hmm,' she moaned, putting her arms round his neck.

An hour later they had both dressed and were ready to go their respective ways. Isabel left first, with Brad standing in the door of the cabin waving her off. When she was out of sight he saddled his own horse that waited in the lean-to and rode up the trail past the trees. Then he took the left fork to Bad Rock. His journey was a troubled one. Isabel's suggestion had shaken him. The last thing he wanted was the complication of a love affair turning into a marriage, even if her father was the richest man around.

He cursed his weakness for the girl, for she was no more than that. Why the hell hadn't he stuck to one of the saloon girls? Suddenly things were getting complicated.

Isabel rode back to her father's ranch in a state of euphoric happiness. Now she felt sure that Brad Fulsom loved her. The only trouble she could see would be her father.

Abe Keller leaned against the hitchrail outside the bunkhouse and watched Isabel ride down the trail. He pulled his hat down and headed for the house. Knocking on the door, he went into the hall and through to the office.

'Miss Isabel's comin' in, boss,' he said to the figure behind the mahogany desk who was scratching away at the ranch accounts.

Lem Forrester did not look up. 'Anybody with her?'

'No, boss. All alone an' in a hurry.' Keller's mouth went dry at the thought of Isabel. Like all the hands, he reckoned her to be a tidy little baggage and like all of the others he knew he would never have a chance with her.

'Your pa wants to see you Miss Isabel,' Keller called over as the girl dismounted.

'Thanks, Abe,' Isabel called back with a politeness she did not feel. As she walked up the steps to the house, she could feel Keller's eyes following her all the way.

She put her hat on the peg just behind the door and went into her father's office. Forrester closed the accounts book and leaned back in the leather swivel chair.

'Now,' he began, 'would you mind telling me where you've been?'

The sharpness of the tone and the question took Isabel aback. She flushed, wondering if her father knew about her and Brad.

'Oh, just riding, Daddy,' she said lightly.

'Come on, who is he?' He snapped the quill pen he had been fidgeting with, his face reddening as he spoke.

'No one, Daddy.' She put on her silkiest tone, the one most calculated to soften up her father. 'I don't know what you mean.'

'Damn it, Isabel, you've had too free a rein since your mother died. I know enough to know when a woman's got herself a man. And you've got yourself a man.' His voice had risen and the colour in his face deepened.

Isabel bit the inside of her mouth. So he knew. Fine. But if he found out it was Brad Fulsom, a saloon owner and gambler, there'd be no telling what he might do.

'You're right, Pa. I have been seeing a man.' She watched as the colour in her father's face lightened. Inwardly, she breathed a sigh of relief.

'Who is he? Not one of these no-account miners that have been drifting into town since they found silver over at Green Creek?' he asked, watching her intently.

'No, Pa,' Isabel told him, her mind seeking some answer to the next inevitable question.

'You going to tell me who he is?' The answer seemed to have mollified him. Then he sat upright in the chair. 'Married, is he?'

Isabel's female instincts told her that it was time to be outraged, to get her pa to change direction. 'Pa, what kind of a girl do you think I am?'

The outrage in her voice took the wind out of Lem Forrester's sails. 'Sorry, darlin', but there's some fellas about these days who wouldn't stop at seducing an innocent young girl.'

Seeing the tear in the corner of her eye, Forrester got up and came round the desk, his meaty hand seeking the calf-skin wallet in his inside pocket. He pulled it out and peeled off a fifty-dollar bill. 'Go into town tomorrow and buy yourself something pretty.'

Isabel flung her arms round her father's

neck and kissed him on the cheek. 'Thanks, Pa.'

She went upstairs feeling pretty well relieved. Good old Pa, she thought, pushing the fifty dollars into the pocket of her skirt.

Eleven

Jed Guthrie led the dead man's horse into Bad Rock, the gunny sack swinging from its pommel.

He watched as Lomax came down the street then called over to him.

'What can I do for you, Guthrie?' he asked.

'Thought you might recognize this hombre and his pal,' Jed said rubbing his aching ankle. 'Made a play at the Lascombes last night. It went wrong.' He pulled up the head of the man he had shot to show to Lomax.

'No, I can't say I've seen him around. Then that don't mean a thing with new folks coming in all the time. Thought you said there was two of them,' he said, patting the muzzle of Jed's horse. Then he gave Jed a puzzled look.

'The other one's in here.' Jed gave a macabre smile pointing to the gunny sack.

'To hell with you, Guthrie. What do you mean?' he asked angrily.

'Blew himself up,' Jed told him coldly.

'I'll take care of it,' Lomax said as he turned to go into his office.

'You done anything about my friends?' Jed asked him.

'Take a look around you, Guthrie. Do I look as though I have that kind of time? This town's filling up faster than either of us can spit,' replied the harassed sheriff. 'Got folks coming in from all over. And most of them a fella couldn't trust his daughter with.'

'That's not something I've got to worry about.' Jed stepped up onto the veranda. 'Maybe you need some help. Like me to ride up and see Lem Forrester?'

'You keep well away from him and his outfit,' Lomax snapped. 'Last thing I need around here is a private war.'

'I'll bear that in mind,' Jed told him.

As Bart Lomax watched Jed walk away, he found it hard to make up his mind about him. He had sent the wire off to the War Department and felt that there was nothing he could do but wait for a reply, but no matter what he felt about Jed Guthrie, he found himself looking for a way to pin a star on that chest.

Mounting the veranda, he went into his office.

'Hi, Sam,' he said to his deputy. 'Just got back?'

'Yeah, just got back and it ain't with any good news, either,' Sam told him sourly.

'Just tell me about it,' Lomax said to his deputy, feeling that all the snow was piling up on his shoulders.

'This some kinda joke, Sam?' Standing in the middle of the office Bart confronted his deputy. Bart had a face like thunder. The news that Sam had brought was bad, and it presented him with another problem.

'No, Bart, it ain't no kinda joke. Seth Wolfram's boys have got a new job down in the valley. Man killer on the loose.'

'So, all they aim to do is drop the silver off at the bank an' leave it here 'til the train to Denver gets in?'

'That's what Wolfram said. Him an' his boys are just gonna make sure it gets down here.' Hutchins grimaced as he stretched. It had been a hard ride up from Pine Gulch and the message he had for Bart hadn't made the ride any easier.

'Go an' get some rest an' something to eat. When you've done, come back here,' Lomax said with a tone of resignation in his voice.

'Sorry, Bart,' Sam mumbled as he went out.

'It ain't your fault,' Lomax told him.

When Sam had gone the door opened and the clerk from the telegraph office came in.

'Hi, Bart. Got that telegram you been waiting for from Washington,' he said, dropping the telegram in front of Lomax.

Eagerly Lomax tore it open and read it.

'Hope it's what you wanted,' the clerk said.

'Yeah,' Lomax told him and watched him go out.

Lomax sat down. The first thing he would need would be some more deputies or a few honest men who were good with a gun, and there were precious few of them about.

Taking a dodger poster out of his desk, Lomax thought for a few minutes. Billy Claibourne, he hesitated. Billy had got a bit long in the tooth, and liked a jug but he could track and he could shoot.

Miles Bennet owned the gunsmith's at the corner of the block. Miles could take the pips out of a playing card. Harry James. He used to be a shotgun guard for the stage line and now ran the office. Lomax wrote down the names. They weren't enough. For a long moment he scratched his head. He wanted one more to be absolutely certain.

As he was about to give up the task for the time being the office door opened and Lomax swung the chair round.

'Hi, Guthrie, what can I do for you this time?' he asked.

'Just going back up to Jilly an' her pa. Just want you to know where you can find me,' Jed told him.

Lomax looked him over. The telegram that the clerk in the telegraph office had delivered told him all he wanted to know.

'Got much dinero on you?' Lomax asked him suddenly.

'Got some, enough to get by. Why, lookin' fer a loan?' Jed smiled.

'Ain't got a job either. An' how long do you think the Lascombes can run to three meals a day?' Lomax stood up.

'I'll move on when I have to,' Jed told him truculently.

'If you ain't got any money and no job, that could make you a vagrant. And that's against the law.' Lomax leaned on his desk.

'And?' Jed asked angrily.

'You'd find it real hard to help me bring in the Murtaghs' killers if you were spending your time in a cell.' He gave Jed a meaningful look.

'You askin' me to help you find those bastards that killed Jack and Lucy?' Jed's voice took on an interested tone.

'Yeah. That and another small chore.' Lomax knew that he had got his fourth man.

'What other "small chore"?' Jed asked suspiciously.

'Just a night's work. You ain't gonna be missed for one night.' Lomax pulled out the makings and offered them to Jed, who took them and started putting them together.

Lomax outlined the job that Seth Wolfram had left them with. ''Course, you'd get regular deputy's pay for it.'

'That'll take some spendin',' Jed said with a laugh as he put a match to the stogie.

'What's it to be? Some pay or some free board and lodging at the town's expense?' Lomax started to roll himself a stogie.

'Got a way with words.' Jed gave a rueful smile.

'Glad you see it that way,' Lomax told him, watching the smoke from Jed's stogie curl upwards.

'Gonna swear me in?' Jed asked with the same smile as before.

'Sure. Raise your right hand,' Lomax told him, pulling a tin star from his desk drawer.

When Jed had raised his hand and Lomax had administered the oath, Lomax pinned on the star.

'This means I'm free to look for Jack and Lucy's killers?' Jed asked.

'Sure does,' Lomax said. 'Just don't forget you're wearing a badge now.'

'Can't see me doin' that,' Jed said with a laugh.

'Git your stuff and move into the jail. But before you do that you'd better come across with me while I tell Jim Anderson what's happening.'

'That's fine with me,' Guthrie said with a satisfied smile. 'And when I've done that, I'll go up and see Jilly and her pa and let them know what's happening.'

Returning to his desk, Lomax pencilled in Jed Guthrie's name with the others.

Twelve

All they had to do then was go over to Jim Anderson and give him the good news.

When they went over to the office, the clerk told them that they would find Anderson in the Lucky Lady.

'That his favourite waterin' hole?' Jed asked as they got outside.

'Jim Anderson keeps a whore in the Lucky Lady an' gets first call on her. A real classy French piece.'

'Hi, Sheriff. Anderson's in his usual room. Don't think he wants to be disturbed, though,' the madam who ran the girls told them as they went in.

Her gaze lingered on Jed for a moment as both men went up the stairs.

'Better get his pants on, then, hadn't

he?' Lomax told her sourly as he clumped up the stairs to Anderson's room.

Lomax rapped hard on the door when he got there. Then, without waiting for an answer, went in, followed by Jed.

As he was sitting up in bed, Jim Anderson's French whore fed him sliced peaches from a spoon. She squealed when both men came in, spilling the thick juice down between the handsome cleavage of her breasts.

With only the bare trace of a smile, Anderson ran his finger up the line of juice and sucked it off the end of his fingers. The whore, Jeanette, squealed again and dropped the spoon with the peach on it onto the bedclothes.

'Next time you knock, Lomax, you wait until I tell you to come in,' he said, shooing Jeanette off the bed.

'I'll bear that in mind,' Lomax told him. 'Just so long as you tell me that Seth Wolfram and his boys aren't paid to hang around until the silver gets on the train so the Wells Fargo boys can ride herd on it down to Denver.'

'Damn it, Lomax, you spoiled my breakfast for that?' Anderson got out of bed and reached for the silk robe that hung over the chair.

Jed got there first and threw it in the air. 'I admire a man who uses the best.' His gaze had travelled to Jeanette who stood by the bed trying to look modest.

'Who's this?' Anderson nodded towards Jed, as he knotted the robe.

'He's a new deputy,' Jed replied. 'An' you can talk to him free of charge. Honest.'

For the first time in a while Bart Lomax felt himself suppress a smile.

'That means there's gonna be a hundred thousand dollars in silver sitting in an empty bank. And I'm gonna be the one that hopes nobody tries to take off with it.' Lomax's voice was high and angry.

'Hell, get the town council to foot the bill for some deputies. They can afford it with all the new revenue coming in.'

Anderson had knotted the tie of the robe.

'It ain't the point, Anderson,' Lomax said as he watched the shapely Jeanette wiping her breasts with a towel.

'What is the point, Lomax?' Snatching the towel from Jeanette, Anderson wiped his pudgy fingers. 'If you ain't up to the job, the council will get somebody who is.'

'Damn it, Anderson. I guess I'll have to. Come on, Jed, let's go see the mayor.'

It took Lomax and hour to persuade Mayor Collins to foot the bill for the extra deputies that he asked for. After that Lomax went around to make sure all the names on the list were willing to help him.

Thirteen

Lomax found Miles Bennet in his shop, cleaning a new .45.

'Be with you in a second, Bart,' he smiled when he saw the sheriff.

'No hurry, Miles. How's the wife and the new baby?' Lomax asked.

'Oh, fine. Got powerful lungs for a little fella,' Miles smiled with all the pride of a new father.

'Glad to hear that. Expect it's costing you plenty extra though. Diapers, food and the like.' Lomax felt like a traitor but time was pressing and he needed those extra guns.

'Yeah, sure is,' Miles said gloomily. 'Costing a fair bit more.'

'Want to make a few extra bucks?' Lomax leaned on the counter.

'How?' Miles asked with interest.

Lomax explained the predicament he found himself in over the silver. 'Just a night's work, then the Wells Fargo boys get it down to the train. That's it.'

For a moment Miles thought about it. 'Got anybody besides Sam and me?'

'Just Sam an' Jed Guthrie, but I'm goin' seein' a few of the boys. Reckon I can come up with a few more names,' Lomax said slowly.

'Hi.' Miles held his hand out for Jed to take.

'Pleased to meet you,' Jed said with a smile.

'OK, I'm in.' Miles wiped his hand on his leather apron and offered it to Lomax.

Starting to feel a heap better, they went down to the office of the stage line to find Harry James. Harry signed up right away for the job.

'Thanks for bearin' me in mind, Bart.

Things are gettin' slack,' he laughed as Lomax left.

'Happen to know if Sam Claibourne's in town?' Lomax asked him before he left the office.

'Losin' his money in Dillon's place last time I saw him,' Harry said as they went out.

'You get the rest of the men together,' Jed told him. 'I'll go up and square things with Barry and Jilly.'

Dillon's was the dirtiest, meanest saloon and whore house in Bad Rock. Lomax had lost count of the number of times he had had to go down there to sort out trouble and he had lost count of the number of times he had threatened to have it closed down.

Eventually, he found Sam Claibourne in the stable round the back sleeping off a night's hard liquor and gambling. Filling a pail from the trough, Lomax emptied it over the head of the sleeping Sam. When it had no effect he filled it again and poured it over the mountain man, who had just started to come to the surface.

'What the hell y'doin', Bart?' he gasped wiping the water out of his eyes and his thick, greasy hair.

Lomax hunkered down beside him. 'We need your help, Sam,' he said before going on to outline his need.

'Over by Saturday mornin' you say? Git paid same day?' Sam's eyes lit up at the prospect of more money to spend at the tables in Dillon's.

'The very same.' Lomax got to his feet. 'Can I count on you?'

'Sure can,' Sam replied as he rolled over and fell asleep once more.

For once Brad Fulsom rode out of Bad Rock not to meet Isabel Forrester, but to meet his informant from Jim Anderson's mine. They were to meet two hours' ride from the mine in the elbow of the river that ran by Pine Gulch. He dismounted and checked his .45, then lit a cigar and settled down to await the arrival of his informant. The cigar was halfway down when he heard the steady plod of a horse making its way over the rocky ground. He got down from the rock he had been sitting on and waited. A rider came round the bend and dismounted.

'Hi, Mister Fulsom,' the man called out as he approached the saloon owner.

'Got what I want, Max?' Fulsom flicked the cigar into the river.

'Sure have. You got what I want?' Max asked greedily.

'Sure.' Fulsom reached into his pocket and produced an envelope containing a wad of greenbacks.

Max took a step forward and reached out for the envelope.

'What's the hurry, Max?' Fulsom gave a twisted grin.

'No hurry, but I'd sure like a sight of all that money.' Max rubbed the front of his trousers with his hands.

Fulsom smiled and pulled the wad out of the envelope and held it under Max's nose. 'See here,' Fulsom rippled the wad of money.

Max almost drooled over the wad. He wiped his thin lips with the back of his hand.

'Your turn now, Max.' Fulsom started to fold the wad up and put it back in the envelope.

'Better than we hoped,' Max said. 'They're bringing the silver into town next Friday mornin'. Wolfram's boys ain't gonna be stayin' with the silver. They got another job, so it's just gonna stay in the bank overnight.'

'You sure about that?' Fulsom asked quickly.

'That's what they wuz tellin' the deputy they sent up to find out what was goin' on,' came the answer. 'Can I have my money now? Don't want to be away too long, otherwise somebody's gonna miss me.' Max looked around quickly as if expecting to see somebody coming up the trail.

'Here,' Fulsom passed over the envelope.

'Thanks, Mister Fulsom. Bin a pleasure doin' business with you,' Max laughed and turned back to where he had tethered his horse.

Fulsom watched him go a few yards, then pulled out his gun. The single shot echoed among the rocks. Max flung his arms out and dropped to the ground.

Breaking open the chamber, Fulsom replaced the shell and retrieved the envelope. Having replaced the envelope in his pocket, Fulsom was about to roll the body into the water when he caught the sound of the hoofs approaching from the trail above.

Jed rode on, his mind set on seeing Jilly once more when the sound of the shot broke his reverie. His gun was instantly in his hand. The clatter of hoof beats on the trail made him urge his horse on more quickly. As he rounded the bend in the trail he caught sight of a horse heading back towards town.

Assuming that a robbery had taken place Jed was just about to go after the supposed assailant when he saw the body of Max lying beside the river. Thinking the man might still be alive, he gigged his horse in that direction, got himself out of the saddle and bent down to examine Max. One look was sufficient to tell him that Max was beyond help. He looked up, but could see no sign of the rider. Whoever it was, he reckoned there was no catching him now.

Rummaging through the pockets he could find nothing that would identify the man. He reckoned that the best thing he could do was to get up to Jilly and tell them that he had a new boss for the time being.

The disappointment was clear to see in the girl's face.

'Just be gone for a day or so. An' this

badge might help me to find the killers,' he told Jilly.

For a moment he hesitated. 'What makes you so sure that Lem Forrester is behind all this?' he asked her.

'He's the only one round here that stands to make anything out of this. No one else is that big, and besides, he's taken a lot of new men onto his payroll. Men who look as though they know the inside of a jail. Real hard cases, not ranchmen,' she said grimly.

'Hope you're sure about that. This Forrester fella might find himself on the wrong end of a rope someday. I hope it's not just female intuition,' Jed grinned.

'No, it ain't just female intuition. Couple of months ago he came up here and made us an offer. When Pa turned him down he got real angry and that's when the trouble started,' she concluded. 'Just you be careful, Jed Guthrie,' she told him, hooking her hands over his head and pulling his face down to hers. 'And mind you come right back.'

Jed felt that she was more concerned with him coming back to see her than keeping Lem Forrester's boys off the property. Jed had decided that the best thing to do would be to tell Lomax what had occurred on the trail and leave it to him.

'I'll go up and tell the boys to expect to be busy.' Glass sat on the edge of Fulsom's desk, nursing a shot of whiskey.

'We got a wagon and team?' Fulsom's voice had an anxious edge to it.

'Sure, we got a wagon and team.' Glass helped himself to another whiskey. 'You're starting to worry.'

'I'm worrying all right. Thought of going back inside makes my guts curl up.' Fulsom had gone white and a sheen had come out on his forehead.

'Don't worry, Brad. Tell you what, why don't you go up and see that little filly of yours and put her through her paces? A romp with a filly always made you feel better.' Glass picked up the bottle and filled out a shot for Fulsom.

'Might just do that. Ride up and leave a note for her. She'll come running. Always does.' He laughed harshly hoping that Isobel had forgotten about weddings and settling down and the like.

'Just one thing you haven't told me,' Glass slipped down from the desk.

'And what's that?' Fulsom asked.

'How do we get the silver out of the bank? Don't think they're gonna hand it over, no matter how polite we ask,' Glass smiled at his confederate.

'Don't think they are,' Fulsom smiled slyly back at him.

'Then share the secret with me.' Glass swallowed the whiskey.

'Been giving the matter some thought, and what the late unlamented Max told me makes it all that much easier. If Wolfram's not going to sleep with the silver, then who is?' Fulsom stopped and waited for Glass. 'It's got to be Lomax with some hired gun from town. And it's my guess that they'll stay in the bank overnight just to be on the safe side.' He wet his lips before going on. 'And that means they'll need some hot chow. It's gonna be damn cold in there.'

'So it's going to be cold in there,' Glass snorted.

'So where do you think this chow's going to come from?' Fulsom's voice had gone hard.

'Charlie Vesty, where else?' Glass sipped at the whiskey.

'Charlie Vesty hell. You ain't been watching,' Fulsom sneered. 'In case you hadn't noticed, Lomax has been getting his food off that pretty little Davies gal.'

'The one whose folks own the general store?' Glass took a cigar from Fulsom's box on his desk and put a match to the end.

'Glad you've seen something besides the cards hitting the table round here,' Fulsom laughed. 'Yeah, that's her. Way I figure it, they'll get some food taken over to the bank by her.' Fulsom helped himself to one of his own cigars and lit it.

'How's that going to help us?' Glass furrowed his eyebrows, trying to follow the point that Fulsom was making.

'Hold them hostage while she takes the food across and put something in it that makes sure they sleep. We wouldn't want them disturbing us would we?'

Glass laughed uproariously. 'Sounds like a damn fine idea to me,' he said, wiping the tears from his eyes.

'Don't it, though?' Fulsom raised his glass. 'Here's to us.'

Fourteen

Jed found the place easy enough. The gate with the burned-in sign over the top proclaimed it loud and clear. He let the horse walk beneath the sign and down the trail into the yard. There was a cluster of buildings with a couple of corrals at the back. One of the buildings stood out. It was better built than the others. And looked painted and cared for. The door opened and a girl came out onto the veranda. A good-looking piece too, he thought to himself.

He aimed the horse towards the veranda, where the girl stood in a split skirt and a white shirt open at the neck with a shoelace tie under the collar.

'Mornin' to you,' he said to her. She gave him a sulky smile.

'Good morning to you, Deputy,' she answered.

'The boss around?' he asked, swinging his leg over the saddle and holding onto the reins.

'The boss?' she asked.

'Yeah, the fella that owns the place, Lem Forrester I think he's called,' he said slowly, making it sound like an insult.

'Oh, Pa,' she replied. Her long eyebrows went up a mite.

'I want to speak to him if he's around.' Jed gave her another long look.

'Yes, he's in. I'll get him.' Her voice was cool, as if she didn't like speaking to him.

She disappeared into the house, leaving Jed to look around the yard. The bunkhouse door opened and a man came out. Jed looked twice. He was the same man he had seen in the alley the day he had ridden up to the Murtaghs' place.

Tying his horse to the rail, Jed walked across the empty yard and came to a stop at the bottom of the steps that led out of the bunkhouse.

'Hi,' Jed said conversationally. 'Seem to know your face from someplace.'

Keller's tongue ran over his dry lips. 'Cain't say same for you,' he replied, his hand crawling towards his gun butt.

Jed slipped the thong over the hammer of his own gun. His finger touched the worn butt of his .45.

'Seem to recollect your face in the alleyway of a certain livery stable that got itself burned down.'

Keller eased the thong over the hammer of his gun.

'You want to call it, you call it, star or no star,' he said.

'Ready to go when you're ready,' Jed's voice was even and slow.

'Keller.' The voice of Lem Forrester cut the air between them. 'Quit that. The both of you.'

Behind him Jed heard the heavy stamp of booted feet crossing the hard-packed earth of the yard.

Forrester now stood between the two men. For a moment there was silence.

'You looking for me?' he turned to face Jed.

'Yeah. And him,' came the cold answer.

'What's your beef?' Forrester met Jed's gaze.

'Stop givin' the folks down in the valley a hard time.' Jed's voice was edged with menace.

'My time's your time, fella,' Keller shouted over Forrester's head.

'Shut it, Keller, or you're riding out of here.' Forrester's face had become mottled and his lips runny with spittle. 'You, whatever your name is, I'm giving nobody down there a bad time and anybody that tells you different is a liar. An' that badge don't give you the right to talk like that. Not while you're on my land,' Forrester shouted, his hand clenching and unclenching at his side.

Jed saw the door of the bunkhouse open

and three mean-looking hombres come out and stand on the veranda. One of them carried a scatter gun and the two others wore their guns tied down. They looked ready to back any play Forrester called.

'There'll be a time for you and Keller.' Jed turned away and walked back to the rail where he had hitched his horse. He had got what he came for and it would not serve his purpose getting gunned down until he had killed or brought to justice those who had murdered his friends.

The girl still stood on the veranda, her hands to her mouth as if trying to hold in a scream. She watched Jed unhitch his horse and climb into the saddle and ride out of the yard without looking back.

'Was you going to put him down in the yard with my daughter watching?' Forrester hit at Keller when Keller came back.

'Hell, boss, thought he was gonna call me then an' there,' Keller said.

'Get it into your head, Keller. I don't

want any killing done hereabouts, especially while my daughter's around. You're going to have to get rid of him. You tried it once. Next time don't let him walk away from it.'

'Don't worry, boss, he won't.' Keller turned and left the office.

Fifteen

Dropping out of the saddle, Jed hitched the mount to the rail outside the sheriff's office.

Inside, Lomax had just finished putting out some of the food that Carol had brought over from the store for his and Sam's supper.

'Plenty for one more,' Carol smiled as Jed came in the door. 'Bart's told me that you've hired on with the others to keep an eye on the silver.'

'Among other things,' he said as he took the mug from Sam who had filled it up with coffee for him.

'Thanks, Sam,' Jed said, raising the steaming mug to his mouth.

'Where've you been, Jed?' Lomax asked from the corner.

'Been up to see Lem Forrester. Mighty interestin' chat I had with him too,' the deputy said, weighing his words.

Lomax's eyes narrowed. 'Hope you ain't been causing trouble,' he said sharply.

'Me cause trouble?' Jed asked innocently. 'No. I've just been having a talk with him an' a couple of his hired hands. One was Keller, I think Forrester called him. Can't say who the other hardcase was. Besides, I'm working for you now.'

'Most likely be Milt Drew,' Sam put in. 'They came up here together last Fall.'

'You been trying to goad Forrester or Keller into making some kind of play?' Lomax asked.

'No. Just asking them to lay off the folks in the valley,' Jed replied.

'If you've got any proof you bring it to me,' Lomax told his new deputy harshly.

'I got all the proof I need right here,' Jed tapped his belly. 'Gut feelin',' he added.

'You work for the law now,' Lomax said.

'For now I'll give it the benefit of the doubt, but if it looks like Forrester's gonna get away with it, then he's mine.' Jed's voice was like a silk scarf.

'You kill anybody without any cause, Jed, an' you'll hang. Badge or no badge, follow what I'm sayin',' Lomax said angrily.

'Follow you real close,' Jed replied.

'Simmer down boys.' Sam Hutchins, seeing a fight brewing, stood up and got between the two of them.

'Sam's right. You boys back off.' Carol intervened. 'You've got enough trouble on your hands,' she said to Lomax.

'The lady's right,' Jed replied in a pacific tone. 'Let it lay for now, we can settle it after we got this silver off our hands.'

Lomax simmered down and an uneasy silence fell over the jail.

Sixteen

Bart Lomax, Sam Hutchins, Jed Guthrie and the others were assembled outside the jail. Just before noon, each of them carrying as well as his side arm, a short-barrelled shotgun.

Lomax stepped to the end of the boardwalk and shaded his eyes against the strong sunlight. At first he could see nothing, then a cloud of dust became apparent down the trail.

'They're comin',' he called out to the others. One by one his deputies ranged themselves in the street, ready for trouble. Seth Wolfram and his boys rode into town, the silver being hauled in on a flat-bed wagon. They reined up outside the bank.

Wolfram sat astride a night-black mare. He was a big man with a long, straggly beard, and he wore a brace of Remingtons. His animal grin, at Lomax, revealed a set of rotting teeth. 'Hi, Lomax. Got somewhere safe to lay this stuff?'

'No, we're gonna leave it out here. Don't think it'll come to any harm,' Lomax told him sarcastically.

Wolfram slid down from his horse. 'Sound a mite pissed off, Lomax,' Wolfram grinned.

'Doin' your job for nothin'd piss anybody off,' Lomax replied as he swung the butt of the shotgun at Wolfram's head.

Big and clumsy he might be, but slow, Wolfram was not. He moved like a stung rattler, his right arm catching the butt of the shotgun before it could land on the side of his head. His grip tightened around the butt, and then he started to edge it backwards, a grin coming over his face.

'Coulda bit off more'n you can chew, Lomax,' he said, wrenching the gun out of the sheriff's grip and flinging it into the trough. His right hand swung sideways, catching Lomax a stunning blow on the side of the head.

Everything in Lomax's vision reeled. He tottered sideways, just catching the hitchrail to prevent himself hitting the dust. His deputies and Wolfram's boys formed a circle round them.

Wolfram rushed at him, his fists flailing like windmill sails. Lomax dropped, and rolled beneath the hitchrail. Grasping it, he pulled himself to his feet and lashed out, striking Wolfram on the kneecap. Wolfram yelled and hobbled backwards. The pain in Lomax's head subsided a mite as he swung under the hitchrail and drove his fist into Wolfram's body. The giant let out a 'whoosh' and folded up.

A crowd of townsfolk had started to gather.

Moving in for the kill, Lomax clenched his fists and brought them down on Wolfram's neck. Wolfram had other plans. Dropping flat, he twisted over onto his back and scythed Lomax's legs from under him.

'Come on, Seth, finish the bastard,' one of his men sang out.

Balancing himself, Wolfram drew back his foot such that, if the kick had landed, it would have sent Lomax's ribs through his lungs. Rolling clear, Lomax scrambled to his feet, bracing himself for Wolfram's rush. Wolfram came blindly on, his face a mask of fury, his arms swinging at Lomax. Dancing to one side, Lomax pushed out his foot, so that Wolfram sprawled over it.

Before Wolfram could recover his balance, Lomax caught him by the scruff of the neck and spun him around, his fists driving into the giant's face until his arms ached. When he let go of Wolfram, Wolfram slid to the ground.

'Next time you say you're gonna do a job here, you do it,' Lomax told the unconscious figure. 'Any of you boys got anything to say?' None of Wolfram's boys had anything to say about it.

'Let's get this stuff unloaded,' Lomax

heard Sam Hutchins say.

The deputies staggered in under the weight of the boxes of silver bars. Harry Drummond, the manager, directed them to the newly built strongroom where it was securely lodged until the following morning. When Drummond was satisfied that it was secure, he left the bank until Monday morning, when he hoped that the silver would be halfway to Denver and no longer a tempting target on his premises.

With the bank manager out of the way, Lomax set his watches for the rest of the day and the night. Two hour shifts, two hours on, and two hours off.

Lomax then went to do the rounds of the bank. When he returned he stood by the window once more. He noticed Brad Fulsom and his partner standing opposite, talking closely together.

'You got it, then?' Fulsom asked his partner. 'Get the boys and the wagon down here by ten, round the back of the bank.'

'They should be sleeping by then. Take the stuff up to the mine and stash it down the tunnel the boys been digging,' Glass recited.

'Right,' Fulsom turned to walk away from his partner.

'What about the boys?' Glass asked.

Fulsom smiled. 'We'll let them put the stuff away nice and tidy like, then bury them with it.'

Glass laughed.

'You got everything ready, Carol?' Les Davies, Carol's pa, called from the living room. His daughter put the cover over the basket that she was going to take over to the jail for the men inside.

'Yes, Pa,' the girl called out. Pulling down the cover she patted it into place just as the door from the yard was flung open.

'Keep quiet, girl,' the masked man said threateningly as he put his hand over her mouth to prevent her from crying out. He waggled the gun under her nose.

Behind him, Carol could see another masked man, his pistol drawn, passing through the kitchen and heading for the living room where her parents were sitting. She heard a muffled cry, then three people came back into the kitchen, the masked man herding two very frightened, pale-faced people in front of him.

'We're not going to hurt you,' Fulsom told the wide-eyed girl. 'Just don't make a sound.' He removed his hand from Carol's mouth.

'What do you want?' she gasped. 'There's no money here.'

'Tie them up,' Fulsom pointed to the elderly couple.

Carol watched as he ushered them out of the kitchen and heard them going upstairs.

'From the looks of things, I'd say you was going to feed them fellas in the bank,' Fulsom said.

'Th ... that's right.' Carol's voice was hoarse and dry.

Reaching into his pocket, Fulsom produced a small phial of clear liquid. 'It's the silver we want, not a rope. This'll put them to sleep 'til morning.'

Fulsom thrust the phial into the girl's trembling hands and watched while she pulled the cover off the food.

'Smells good,' he chuckled. 'Put it in the coffee.'

With trembling hands, Carol took out the stopper and poured the liquid into the pot.

Taking the phial from her, Fulsom returned it to his pocket. He waited a moment, while Glass came down. 'Everything all right up there?' he asked.

'Fine and dandy,' Glass said.

'OK, little lady, we're going to take a walk over to the bank. I'll be waiting across the street. You blow the whistle and you get a bullet, then I come back here and two more people get it.' From the tone of his voice and the look in his eyes, Carol could see that he meant what he said.

Taking her bonnet from behind the door and putting it on, she went out through the store. On the boardwalk she hesitated, trying to think of a way of raising the alarm without getting anybody killed.

Fulsom nudged her in the back with his .45.

She stepped off the boardwalk and started down the street towards the bank. At the start of the block where the bank stood, Fulsom caught her by the shoulder.

'Remember, I'll be right here.' His voice was menacing.

Taking a gulp of fresh air, Carol began to walk towards the bank. It seemed a long way, and this part of the town was quiet and still. She felt afraid.

Going up the steps to the bank, she waited a moment, hoping for some idea to come to her. Nothing came. She knocked softly on the door.

The shade was pulled back and Sam Hutchins' face peered through the glass.

It broke into a grin as he recognized her.

Carol heard the bolts being drawn and the lock clicking. The door swung open. Jed brushed past her, his shotgun covering the street. Carol went into the bank and closed the door behind her.

Miles Bennet sniffed his appreciation as Carol pulled the cover off the food. He hadn't been eating too well since his wife had given birth to his son.

'How's things out there?' Lomax asked her, nodding towards the street.

Carol's mouth tightened. She wanted desperately to tell her fiancé the truth but she was afraid of what might happen to her parents if she did.

'Pretty quiet,' she managed to say.

'Say, you ain't sickening for something are you?' Sam Claibourne asked her, cutting into a piece of chicken pie.

'I noticed that,' Lomax said. 'You feeling all right?'

Carol put her hand on her heart. 'What makes you say that?'

'Dunno,' Sam replied. 'You look kinda pale.'

'Oh, I'm all right,' she told them, as she put the cloth back over the basket.

'I'll walk you back,' Lomax said, attempting to take the basket from her.

'Oh, no, Bart,' she stammered. 'It isn't far and there won't be any trouble.'

'No trouble for me,' Bart insisted, taking the basket from her.

Sam Claibourne opened the door to let them out into the night. Carol felt that they could hear her heart beating. She resolved that at the first sign of trouble, she would tell Bart everything.

From the corner, Brad Fulsom watched the couple emerge from the bank. He swore viciously beneath his breath. Then he calmed down. He watched them coming in his direction, then realized that it would be funny if Lomax didn't see his girl home.

He cut down the alley and sheltered behind some trash. They crossed a few yards away, Lomax with his arm on Carol's shoulder. Fulsom could see nothing to worry about. Ducking down the alley he travelled parallel to them.

'Gonna invite me in for some coffee?' were the words that Carol had dreaded to hear.

'Sorry, Bart, but Pa's not too good. Stomach's been troubling him and he's gone for an early night,' she said sombrely. 'Besides, shouldn't you be getting back to that silver?'

'Suppose so,' he replied a little disconsolately. 'You sure you're feelin' all right?'

Putting her hands on his shoulders, Carol kissed him quickly and went inside the store, before he could say anything.

'Damn strange,' Lomax said to himself.

Fulsom had crossed the street behind Lomax and Carol and was now standing in the alley opposite, his .45 cocked and ready.

For a moment, Lomax stood looking up and down the street. Then he turned and headed back to the bank.

'Everythin' OK?' Harry James asked, as Lomax went into the bank.

'Dunno. Think something's wrong with Carol,' he said, then shrugged. 'More likely one of them women's things.'

Harry offered him a piece of the chicken pie and filled out a mug of coffee. Around him, Lomax could see that the others were sitting quietly around the manager's desk, where the deck of cards lay fanned out on the table. Claibourne and Hutchins were lying on the floor, their mouths open as they snored noisily.

'Hope we're not going to have to listen to that every time they take a nap,' Jed grinned.

Drinking half of the coffee in the mug, Lomax sat down to eat the chicken pie.

'Did really well, missy,' Fulsom said through the thick hood that covered his face.

'Your turn now,' Matt Glass poured out

a cup of coffee for her and tipped the last of the sleeping draught into the mug.

'I hope they catch you before you spend a red cent of that money,' she breathed.

'I expect they'll try, but they'll be looking in all the wrong places,' Glass laughed.

Determinedly, Carol put the mug to her mouth and drank the tasteless potion down in one swallow.

'Best sit down.' Fulsom caught her by the elbow and guided her back into the living room and down onto the sofa.

'Sleep tight, pretty thing. We'll be gone before you waken up.'

'Come on, let's go,' Fulsom urged his partner when Carol had closed her eyes.

The two men moved through the alleys until they reached the rear of the saloon. There they found Garrett and the others with a buckboard that they had kept in hiding for this moment.

'Let's git,' Fulsom whispered, leading the horses down to the rear of the bank.

It did not take Art Kenny long to break

the locks on the window and get in. Once inside, he quickly opened the back door for the others.

'Don't that look sweet?' Blaine said, as he looked at the men sprawled out on the floor.

'We'll look sweet if we're still here when they wake up.' Fulsom pulled Blaine to the strongroom where Garrett had already started on the lock.

'Ain't gonna take long, is it?' Fulsom asked quietly.

'No, we'll be out of here before they've finished dreamin',' Garrett said.

He hunched over the safe and went back to work.

The others stood round watching him, their palms sweating as he manipulated the tumblers. After what seemed the hell of a long while the safe door swung open. He heard the others breathe a sigh of relief.

'OK, you jackasses, let's git this place cleared out,' Garrett sneered.

They started to carry the boxes out to

the wagon and load them. Blaine and Kenny remained on the wagon to tie down the boxes.

'That's the last one,' Fulsom said, hurrying out to the wagon. 'Let's git.'

Seventeen

So great was the rush to get out of town that none of the men saw Al Fryer lurching out of an alley.

'The hell with you an' your cheap saloon, Fulsom,' Al Fryer squawked, having just been thrown out of Fulsom's place, his dinero having recently run out.

The wagon and its cargo lurched on up the rough trail towards the mine where the gang intended hiding it. For a second its wheels spun in mid-air as it came close to going over a ravine.

'Go easy, Garrett,' Blaine shouted out as the wagon lurched violently.

'You wanna drive?' Garrett called back, as he lashed the horses once more.

Fulsom hung on as best he could. The wagon was shaking about all over the trail, and he was afraid of being catapulted into space.

'Don't worry,' Glass told him. 'I'll spend your share.'

Glass led Fulsom's horse behind the wagon.

'You're gonna blow those horses before we're anywhere near,' Blaine yelled over the sound of the wagon being thrown from side to side.

'They'll make it all right,' Garrett called to him.

He was right. Half an hour later, Garrett hauled the team to a standstill by the cabin.

Badly shaken Fulsom got down. 'Better throw this stuff in the mine,' he said, throwing a glance at Glass, who understood what he meant.

'You givin' us a hand?' Blaine asked them.

'Guess so,' Glass replied as Blaine cut one of the ropes that secured the load.

Between them, they carried the boxes

into the mine entrance.

'Take them right in,' Fulsom said. 'We don't want nobody falling over them.'

'Sure as hell we don't,' Garrett said, feeling for a match to strike against the wall so that he could light one of the lamps inside the cave entrance.

Fulsom and Glass hung back while the others carried the boxes of silver deeper into the mine. When the last one had been carried in, they followed their men inside.

'Looks like that's the last one,' Blaine said, turning to face Fulsom and Glass.

'Sure is for you boys,' Glass told them, drawing his gun.

'You double-crossing bastards,' yelled Blaine, reaching for his own gun.

'S'long boys. It's been nice working with you,' Fulsom told him as he squeezed the trigger.

The shots boomed down the narrow mine shaft, the flashes from the guns illuminating the scene. One by one the men fell backwards, blood pumping from the holes in their bodies.

'Downright decent of them boys,' Glass said. 'Not wanting any farewell party or nothing like that.'

'Can't get help like that no more,' Fulsom laughed. Fulsom led the team and the wagon further into the cave where he shot the horses.

On their way out, they pulled some logs over the entrance just to discourage anybody from taking a closer look.

Fulsom and Glass were just having their second cup of coffee along with an extra helping of ham and eggs when Lomax and his deputies started coming round in the empty bank.

Lomax got his head up off the manager's desk, feeling like he'd been on an all-night drinking spree. Then he stood up. For a moment he stood behind the desk trying to figure out what had happened. A cold feeling seeped through his six-foot frame.

He lurched into the corridor where he found Sam Hutchins coming from the outer office, rubbing his head.

'Bin down to the safe yet?' Sam asked.

'No. I'm headed there now,' Lomax said.

He felt sick when he saw the open safe minus its contents. He felt the bile rise in his throat.

'Jim Anderson's gonna have your hide,' Sam said comfortingly.

'Our hides,' Lomax's voice sounded real sour.

'OK, our hides,' Sam replied.

The other deputies were in a similar fix when Lomax went in to them. They woke up one by one, their heads thick and their mouths crusty dry.

'We gonna draw lots for who tells Anderson?' Claibourne asked.

'I ain't doin' it,' Jed put in.

'Nobody's asking you to,' Lomax said, biting his head off.

'Somebody's gonna have to go,' Harry

James said as he swallowed a glass of water from a pitcher on the desk.

'You got it, Sheriff,' Guthrie said.

'Yeah, I've got it.' Lomax pulled on his stetson and unlocked the door.

It was early enough for the street to be empty. He found Anderson where he had found him before. Sporting with his French whore.

'What hell's going on, Lomax?' Anderson's voice was angry. The whore had not really woken up yet.

'Bank's been cleaned out,' Lomax said embarrassedly.

'This is no time to be joking, Lomax,' Anderson said, slapping the whore's rump as she started to waken up.

'This is no joke, Anderson,' Lomax replied.

'What, it's gone with you and your boys looking after it?' Hopping out of bed, Anderson reached for his clothes. 'Damn it, Lomax, how'd it happen? Didn't hear any shooting.' Anderson had pulled on his shirt and was wrestling with his pants, his suspenders hanging down by his side.

'Not right sure, but I guess we were drugged.' An embarrassed silence hung in the air.

'Who? How?' Anderson gobbled red-faced, like a turkey looking at an axe.

'Only way I can figure it is—well, Carol brought us some chow down. Guess it must have been in that.'

'Lomax, are you saying Carol was in on this?' Anderson stared at the sheriff, his eyes wider.

'No—No. I don't know what I'm saying. I'm gonna go down and talk to her about it.' Pulling on his stetson, Lomax headed for the door.

He walked quickly down the stairs and into the street. With each step he felt himself walking faster, so that by the time he got there he was practically running.

Lomax went round to the back door and found it open. He drew his Colt and pushed inside to find Carol and her

165

parents standing in the kitchen, looking thick-headed.

'You all right?' he asked quickly.

'Yes, Bart, and thanks for coming over so quickly. It was terrible,' Carol gasped, hugging Lomax, who had put away his gun.

When he had made sure that everything was all right, Bart hurried back to the jail, where he found Jed and Billy Claibourne waiting for him.

'Let's check round the back of the bank,' Lomax said as he, Billy and Jed went out. 'Way I figure it, they must have had a wagon to get it out of town.'

They went around to the rear of the bank and found what they were looking for, a set of fresh wheel marks heading for Main Street.

'Let's get the horses and see where these marks take us,' Lomax said eagerly.

The three men went around to the barn that the council was using as a livery stable until a new one was built.

Lomax stopped when they got back with the horses and looked at the ground. The number of people moving out of town and up to the diggings had made it impossible to tell one set of marks from another.

Billy looked at him. 'What do we do now?' he asked.

'Let's see if we can pick 'em up just outside town.'

Lomax urged the horse on towards the edge of town. The story was just the same there. Just a mess of tracks of all kinds that made sorting out one set from another impossible. For an hour they struggled with the task before finally giving it up.

No man saw the smirk on Brad Fulsom's face as he was taking the air with Matt Glass.

'Sick of chasing their tails already,' he said to Glass.

'Didn't take them long, did it?' Glass lit a cigar.

Both men went back inside, feeling that

they had earned an extra breakfast after their night's work.

'What the hell do you mean, you lost them?' Mayor Coleman bellowed at Lomax and his deputy.

'I mean just that,' Lomax stood his ground. 'There's that many sets of tracks leading everywhere out there that it's impossible to spot the ones we want.'

'Both our jobs are on the line,' Coleman said harshly.

'Yeah, I kinda guessed they would be,' Lomax said bitterly. 'I'll take Billy Claibourne down the Denver trail. Reckon that must be the only place they'd take it.'

'You do that, Bart. You do that very thing.' Coleman picked up his pen and started to scratch at his ledger again.

'OK if I ride up and see that Jilly and Barry are all right?' Jed asked Lomax when they got back to the office.

Bart went out and gave Sam Hutchins and Billy the good news. 'I want you to stay here, Sam,' he told his deputy.

'Anything you say, Bart,' Sam replied, watching the two men mount up.

They rode in silence down the Denver trail, their eyes on the ground beneath them. They rode for two hours, noon having come and gone. Finally, discouraged by the fruitless search, Lomax and Billy Claibourne turned back to town.

'Jed's been in, wants to know if he can do anything to help, besides stay away from Lem Forrester? He's down gettin' some eats,' Sam greeted them.

'Tell him to git back here in the morning,' Bart said, 'and we'll give the whole area a good going over.'

'Right, Bart,' Sam said.

The following morning, Bart Lomax, Jed Guthrie, Sam Hutchins and Billy Claibourne searched up and down, with the only things to show being short tempers and big appetites.

Lomax flung his stetson down on his

desk when he got in. The robbery had started to turn into a nightmare. It was as if the silver had disappeared into thin air, along with the gang who had stolen it. The four men sat about in silence.

'If you boys want to get some chow you can tell Charlie Vesty the town's paying.' Lomax sounded real disappointed and pissed off.

Eighteen

Lomax was having a busy night. Along with Sam Hutchins he had gone down to two saloons to break up trouble, leaving Jed to take care of the prisoners that were filling up the cells. Now, the three of them were in the office, with full cells just down the corridor.

Sam was just fixing some coffee when the door opened and a barman from the Silver Palace came in, all breathless and wind-blown.

'What is it?' Lomax had just picked up his mug.

'Got some trouble down at the Silver Palace,' the man blurted out.

Lomax took a long pull at the coffee. 'Not something we get every night, is it boys?' he asked wearily.

'Sure ain't,' Sam laughed, taking a pull at his coffee.

'OK fella,' Lomax finished his drink and put the mug down on the pot-bellied stove.

'Thanks, Sheriff,' the barman said.

'C'mon Sam, let's take the air. Jed, you take care of things here,' Lomax said as he went out.

They went outside. The town had quietened down considerably. Only a few citizens were out on the streets and most of them seemed to be looking for their beds.

When the sheriff and his companion got down to the Silver Palace, they found that a crowd had gathered around the batwings.

Lomax pushed his way through. When he got inside, he found Brad Fulsom standing over the body of Al Fryer. Lomax got real angry.

'Give me that,' he said as he snatched the gun from Fulsom's hand.

He hunkered down beside Al, whose shirt front was soaked in blood. Reaching out, Lomax put his hand on Al's neck. For a moment he said nothing, then he stood up.

'Somebody get a doctor.' From the corner of his eye he saw the colour drain from Fulsom's face.

Someone scurried from the back of the saloon and moments later, Lomax saw the batwings swinging as they opened and closed.

'What happened?' he asked Fulsom.

Fulsom went dry mouthed. 'He came in. He'd already had enough some place else. Started demanding more,' Fulsom said. 'When Joe said he couldn't have any he got mad and pulled a gun. He fired first. Ain't that right?' Fulsom looked around for support.

'Yeah, that's right,' drawled Matt Glass from somewhere in the crowd.

'And where were you?' Lomax asked.

'Just coming in from the office,' Glass

jerked his thumb over his shoulder.

Studying the layout, Lomax knew that Glass could be telling the truth, but seeing how many people were in the place he doubted if he had a clear view of things.

'Anybody else see what happened? Come on, sing out,' he said, watching the faces of the people in the bar.

The batwings swung open and Tom Dailey, the town barber, came in.

'Where's Doc Medgrave?' Lomax asked quickly.

'Out at Lem Forrester's place,' Tom said, dropping down to examine Al.

'What's he doing there?' Lomax demanded.

'Seein' to a shootin',' Tom replied. 'Somebody's put a bullet in Lem.'

'They picked a damn fine time to do it,' Lomax barked.

'Some of you boys gonna give me a hand gettin' Al down to my shop?' Tom Dailey asked those around him.

Eventually, four of them got a blanket

and put Al in it, then carried him down to the barber's shop on Main Street.

'Any idea what happened at Lem's place?' Lomax cornered Tom when they got down to the barber's shop.

'No, they just sent somebody down for a doc. Think Isabel had somethin' to do with it,' Tom said as they laid Al out on a table in the back room. 'But yer new deputy seemed awful interested.'

'I'll bet he did,' Lomax said.

'Yeah. He was at the bank the night it got emptied.' Tom reddened when he realized what he had said. 'Sorry, Bart, I didn't mean any offence.'

'No offence taken, Tom,' Lomax said, feeling uncomfortable. 'Anybody else go up there besides Jed and the doc?'

'No, just them two.' Tom opened the front of Al's shirt. 'Looks worse than it is,' he said. 'Gonna be unconscious for a spell, though,' he added, getting to work.

While Lomax waited in the barber's shop, the Silver Palace played out the night and was slowly emptying.

Fulsom and Glass were in the back room opening a fresh bottle. 'What's eating you, Brad?' Glass poured Fulsom another drink.

'Think we ought to get the stuff and run,' Fulsom said shakily.

'It's safe where it is. You said so yourself,' Glass replied, taking a sip of the brandy.

'That fella I shot, he knows about what we did, an' he's gonna tell Lomax. Told me just after he went down.' The sweat had broken out on Fulsom's forehead. His hand trembled a mite.

'We ain't gonna do anything about it,' Glass told him.

'This is different. We ought to go up there, get the silver and get outta here,' Fulsom said.

'That'd be damn foolish,' Glass's face curled up angrily. 'You said so yourself.'

'Maybe I was wrong.' Fulsom's hand shook as he spoke.

'I say you weren't.' Glass finished the brandy and started on a refill.

Fulsom's eyes narrowed as he saw the years in the Pen stretch endlessly out, if he didn't get a rope. He wasn't going back to jail.

'Brad, what's the matter with you?' Glass shouted.

'I'm going up there for my share. And don't try and stop me.' Fulsom had stood up, the brandy from the upturned glass disappearing into the carpet.

'Figurin' to run out on me?' His partner stood up, the chair falling over behind him.

Fulsom dived at him from the other side of the desk.

Both went down in a tangled heap. They kicked and clawed at each other. Fulsom got to his feet and reached for the brandy bottle behind him. Twice he brought it down heavily on the head of his partner.

Fulsom put the bottle down on the desk.

He knew that he had to get out of town quick.

One by one he doused the lamps in the office, then let himself out into the corridor.

The street was empty when he came out of the alley. Carefully, he cat-footed along until he came to the barn where he had stabled his horse. Saddling up, he walked the animal quietly to the edge of town and mounted up.

Lomax watched Fulsom from the cover of some buildings near the Silver Palace. If Al Fryer had not come to for a couple of minutes and started wandering about some wagon that Fulsom had been riding on that had nearly cut him in two on the night that the bank had been robbed, Lomax might have gone back to the jail for some coffee and an hour with his head down at his desk before the town started to surface with the dawn. As it was Lomax had decided to play a hunch. He had waited in the shadows around the saloon and followed

Fulsom while he had saddled his horse. Then, he had saddled his own horse. It was a better than even bet that Fulsom was panicking and going to pick up his share of the silver. Once he had done that Lomax could return to Bad Rock and pick up his partner.

Nineteen

Isabel Forrester had come to a decision. She could no longer stay away from the man whom she loved and who she believed loved her.

She and her father had dined in an uncomfortable silence, with her feeling his suspicious glances on her every time she raised her fork to her mouth.

'Is something wrong, Pa?' she asked finally, as Pedro, the cook, brought in coffee from the kitchen.

'No, Isabel, nothing is wrong,' he told her. 'Should there be?'

Pedro filled out Lem Forrester's cup for him, did the same for Isabel, then retired to the kitchen.

'No, Pa,' she hesitated before going on. 'It's just that you seem on edge this evening.'

'There's nothing wrong with me, I can assure you.' He dropped a spoonful of sugar into the coffee and stirred it without taking his eyes off her.

For Isabel, that settled the matter. Her father knew about her and Brad. He had made it clear that he did not want Brad Fulsom in his house again, that inviting him for drinks had merely been the returning of a courtesy that Fulsom had extended when he had opened his saloon.

Isabel's mouth dried. Her small, pink tongue touched her lips.

'If you'll excuse me, Pa, I've suddenly developed a headache.' Quickly, she got up from the table and hurried upstairs.

She closed the door of her room and went over to the window to sit at her dressing table. If her pa knew about her and Brad there was no knowing what he would do. He would probably have Abe Keller and Milt Drew make sure that Brad never came near her, or any other woman, again.

From her window she watched a couple of hands walking slowly back to the bunkhouse after settling their mounts in the stable. One of them was Abe Keller. As he reached the steps of the bunkhouse, he turned and looked up at her window. When he reached the door, he turned and looked up at her window again. She could not see herself spending her life on the same range as men like Keller and Drew. She smiled. She would go down and speak with Pa. He would see reason. She would tell him what she had found out about the Murtaghs. That would be enough. After that she would marry who she liked, but it would be Brad.

Bracing herself, Isabel went out of the room and stood on the landing for a moment, then she went down the stairs. Her father sat in a leather-covered chair, a glass of brandy resting on one of the arms. His face was flushed with the drink.

'Pa,' she said, standing by his side.

Lem Forrester turned sharply. 'Yes, Isabel.'

'Pa,' she began. 'It's about Brad Fulsom.'

'That two-bit gambler?' he asked angrily.

'Yes, Pa.' Isabel could feel herself trembling as her father's face turned scarlet. 'I love him,' she said with an effort.

Forrester practically jumped out of his chair. The drink fell from the arm, the newspaper he had been reading crumpled as his hand whitened and clenched around it.

'Fulsom? You love Brad Fulsom?' His voice was wild with shock and rage.

'And I'm going to marry him,' came the defiant reply.

Her fear of her father had suddenly disappeared, she felt as angry as he looked.

'Marry him?' came the echoed reply.

'Yes, Pa.' Isabel braced herself for it. 'And there's nothing you can do about it,' she shouted at him.

'I can do a lot about it, young lady,' he stormed.

'I know what Abe Keller and Drew did to the Murtaghs.'

'That ain't any of your business, Isabel.' He calmed a little.

'Bart Lomax might not see it that way,' she snapped.

Lem Forrester's face became ashen. 'What are you saying, Isabel?'

'I'm saying that I'm going to marry Brad Fulsom, and there's nothing you can do about it.' Her voice had quietened and steadied.

'I've not built up this ranch just for it to end up in the hands of somebody like Brad Fulsom.' His voice had become savage as he spoke.

'I don't care why you built this ranch up,' Isabel spoke quietly, her voice under control. 'I'm going to marry Brad Fulsom.'

He caught her by the shoulders and shook her. 'No, you aren't,' he gasped.

Thrusting her hand into his chest, Isabel pushed her father away. His face had screwed up into a mask of hatred. Reeling back across the room, he staggered into the office.

'Pa, I'm going to marry him,' Isabel screamed as she took a couple of steps forward, but Lem grasped for the handle of the drawer, which he pulled open. In the drawer lay his .45. He snatched it up and brandished it at Isabel.

'I'm not going to let you throw yourself away on a skunk like Brad Fulsom,' he raged.

'Pa,' screamed Isabel. She ran towards him, her mind intent on Brad Fulsom. She grabbed the pistol and crashed into her father. Both of them fell against the desk as the gun roared.

Charlie Gates had been the last of the hands to get into the ranch yard that night and had fixed up his horse into the livery before going for some chow. Charlie was just opposite the ranch house when he heard the shot.

He ran up the wooden steps and into the ranch house. From the corridor he could see Isabel standing over her father, the smoking gun in her hand. Lem lay on the floor by the desk, blood coming out of a hole in his chest.

'Glory be,' he said, taking the smoking gun from Isabel, whose eyes were glazed and uncomprehending.

Sitting her down in a chair, Charlie said, 'I'll go over to the bunkhouse and send somebody over here to look out fer yer. Then I'll go into town fer the sheriff.'

Isabel nodded without saying anything.

Charlie Gates ran across to the bunkhouse where he found most of the crew playing cards.

'Best git over there,' he pointed to the ranch house.

Jack Ginley the ramrod, looked up in surprise from his hand. 'What the hell's bitin' you?' he asked Charlie.

'The boss's got a bullet in him, an' it looks like Miss Isabel done it,' he gasped out.

Keller and Drew exchanged glances.

'I'm goin' fer the sheriff an' Doc Medgrave.' With that Charlie went to saddle his horse.

He rode as fast as he could down the darkened trail, only pausing to let his horse catch its breath on the edge of town. Jumping down from the saddle, he hitched his horse and went into the sheriff's office.

'Where's the sheriff?' Charlie Gates gasped out, seeing Jed whittling at a piece of wood.

'Gone over to the Silver Palace. Been some trouble.' Jed looked up from his whittling, sensing trouble.

Quickly, Gates told him what he knew.

'Get Doc Medgrave. I'll see you up there,' Jed said, anxious that Forrester did not die before he spoke to him and anxious that Keller and Drew did not disappear.

The trail was empty and he encountered no living soul until he rode into the yard of Forrester's ranch. Seeing a light on in the bunkhouse he left his horse and went over to the house.

'Bring a doctor?' Jack Ginley asked as soon as Jed walked in.

'No, but Doc Medgrave's coming up,' Jed told him.

Looking around the assembled hands and not seeing Keller any place, he asked, 'Where's old man Forrester?'

Ginley indicated the upstairs with a nod of his head. 'Isabel's with him, but she don't seem right in the head somehow. Keeps goin' on about runnin' off with Brad Fulsom. Can't make head nor tail of it.'

'I'm going up,' Jed told Ginley. 'See if I can get any sense out of any of them.'

'In case you wuz wonderin', Keller and Drew are in the bunkhouse,' Ginley told him.

Jed remembered Ginley as one of the hands who had come out of the bunkhouse when he confronted Forrester and Keller.

'Ol' Lem's bin goin' too far,' he said,

guessing why Jed had come to the ranch.

'Thanks,' the deputy said as he started to take the stairs two at a time.

He found Lem Forrester stretched out in a double bed in the front room, his colour all but gone, his breathing coming in wheezy gasps. Isabel sat in a rocking chair beside the bed, humming quietly to herself.

'Don't look as though you've got long, Forrester. Care to ease your conscience?'

'Guess I might as well. If only the Murtaghs hadn't been so damn stubborn an' just got out, none of this would have happened.' He laughed so that the frothy red blood ran down his chin. 'Guess you'll be wantin' a word with Keller and Drew. They pulled the triggers.' A bout of coughing raked him, sending more frothy red bubbles down his chin.

'Forrester, you bastard.' Jed suddenly realized he was shaking a dead man.

He stepped back and looked down at the corpse.

'He's dead.' He turned to face Isabel. 'Your pa's dead,' he repeated.

Isabel looked past him, out through the window.

'It doesn't matter,' she said, rocking steadily in her chair. 'Brad's coming for me.'

For a moment Jed stared at the girl, then he realized that whatever the truth about what had happened that night, her mind had given way under the strain and he did not think that she would ever tell anybody.

Quietly, he went downstairs and found Ginley helping himself to a glass of Forrester's best brandy. Ginley stopped suddenly when he saw Jed.

'Thought you might want a drink,' he said shamefacedly.

'Get one for yourself,' Jed told him, as he took the glass. 'Might as well get two. Lem Forrester'll have no more use for it.'

It took a second before it sunk into Ginley's brain.

'Dead is he?'

'Could say that.' Jed drank the brandy.

Ginley raised his glass in a toast.

'Go over to the bunkhouse and tell Keller and his pal that I'm coming for them. I'm taking them in dead or alive, it's their choice.'

Ginley licked his lips and then he went out. Jed heard his boots on the wooden boards outside.

The big clock on the wall ticked and the pendulum swung as Jed waited for Ginley to return.

He heard the house door open, and Ginley's footsteps in the hall.

'They'll meet you in the yard.' Ginley reached out for the bottle and the glass. Jed noticed that Ginley's hand was shaking.

No lamplight shone from the bunkhouse, but a full moon illuminated the yard of the ranch with the corrals behind the bunkhouse. Two figures came off the bunkhouse veranda.

Moving in their direction, Jed eased the

thong from over the hammer of his gun.

'Lem's dead, boys. It's your turn now, unless you want to come in and tell it to a jury,' he called out to the figures a few yards away.

'You're gonna be givin' Lem some company,' Keller called back as he and Drew moved a few more paces apart.

Jed watched them for a few seconds, figuring Keller to be the faster of the two. As his hand dropped to his gun, Jed fell on his face and rolled to his left, firing as he did so. Keller screamed as the slug tore into his guts. His legs buckled and he dropped his gun so he could clutch his belly, blood spilling through his fingers. He went down on his face.

Milt Drew fired. His bullet winged inches over Jed's head as he took another roll and fired while he was on his back. The bullet from the .45 smashed through the bone of Drew's skull, flinging him backwards into the dust of the yard.

Slowly, Jed got to his feet and looked

at the two bodies for a moment. Behind him he heard the boards creak.

'Get 'em, then?' Ginley asked, emptying another glass of Forrester's brandy down his throat.

'Yeah, I got them,' Jed said quietly.

Twenty

Lomax did not find it hard to follow his quarry up the moonlit trail. Fulsom seemed to have no suspicion that he was being followed. The jingle of his mount's harness sounded clearly down the trail.

Once or twice, Lomax thought that he had lost Fulsom, but each time the sound of the harness came back to him and the shape of the man could be made out just ahead, or silhouetted against the skyline.

At the top of a rise, he recognized the Lascombe place below him. The lights in the cabin were out. Fulsom swung his horse out east, skirting Lem Forrester's place. Lomax wondered how Jed was faring in town, but Jed was a big boy, who seemed more than capable of looking after himself.

Fulsom's route puzzled him. There was nothing in this part of the country but played-out mines or mines that had been abandoned by those who had just lost heart and moved on. A cold wind prowled through the trees, snapping at Lomax's face and fingers. Despite his thick jacket, he shivered. The moon showed Fulsom to be swinging off the main trail. A side trail pushed through the trees and when Lomax swung onto it, he saw the marks of wagon wheels. Judging by their depth, Lomax reckoned that the wagon had been pretty heavily loaded.

As silently as he could, Lomax pushed on. He could not see Fulsom. For a moment he stopped at the side of the trail. A cold silence hung on the air. Something stirred up ahead. A light flickered in the dark.

Dismounting, Lomax tethered his horse and drew his .45. The light grew and Lomax could see that Fulsom had lit a lamp. The figure of Fulsom, the lamp held in front of him, moved into a cave. Lomax moved in after him.

The shadows in the cave danced from side to side as the wind whipped the flame in the lamp. They had started around a long bend when Fulsom stopped and turned round. Lomax stopped as well. Beyond Fulsom, Lomax could see the boxes with the silver in them. Beside them lay something which he could not at first make out. Then Fulsom turned back again and moved on, shedding more light on what lay beside the boxes. Lomax could make out the bodies of what he figured was the rest of the gang.

'Thanks, Fulsom,' he said, stepping out of the shadows.

Fulsom turned, his face was the colour of wax.

'Didn't think you had the brains to stash it here. Know I wouldn't. Reckon there's a rope waiting for you when we get back. They your buddies?'

Fulsom flung the lamp at Lomax then

threw himself at the startled sheriff. The lamp struck the pistol, sending the shot high into the roof of the cave. Sheriff and outlaw sprawled among the rocks and dust.

Fulsom fought like the cornered rat that he was, and Lomax found the .45 knocked from his grasp and heard it go skittering across the tunnel. Both men rained blows on each other. Fulsom reached out and got his hand round a fair-sized rock. Viciously, he brought it down on Lomax's head.

Lomax felt sick as the world turned somersaults. His stomach rose to his throat as Fulsom groped around in the dark for the pistol. As Lomax struggled to his feet, Fulsom's hand fell on the gun.

'Looks like you're gonna die a rich man, Sheriff,' he said as he cocked the .45.

As his finger curled round the trigger, the roof above him groaned and tore itself apart. Rocks and dust fell like a vengeful storm on Fulsom, burying him where he stood.

Staggering back, Lomax turned and lurched from beneath the deluge, and out into the night as the mine started to fill up.

For a while, he sat on a rock outside the mine, gulping in the air. 'Gonna take you some time and some money to dig that out, Anderson,' he said as he climbed into the saddle.

It had started to get light as he rode into Bad Rock, his ribs still aching from the desperate beating that he had taken from Fulsom.

When he had hitched up his horse he climbed the steps to the office. Jed and Sam were nursing some coffee when he went in.

'One of the bartenders has been over. Found Matt Glass in the office, had his head beat in,' Sam told his boss.

'Guess it must have been Fulsom,' Lomax said quietly.

'Looks like some kinda storm took a dislike to you.' Sam got up to pour Lomax a mug of coffee.

'Something like that,' Lomax said, then went on to tell them about what had happened up at the mine.

Sam handed him the mug of coffee.

'What's all this about a shooting up at Lem Forrester's place?' He looked at Jed.

Jed eased himself into the chair and told the sheriff what had occurred up at Lem Forrester's.

'You sure Keller and Drew shot the Murtaghs?' Lomax asked, wrapping his hands around the mug.

'Yeah, old Lem told me before he died. And I gave them an even break, which is more than they gave Jack and Lucy.' He looked up at Lomax. 'Told them they could come in and tell it to a jury or ....' He left the rest unsaid.

'And they made a stupid choice,' Sam interjected.

'And they made a stupid choice,' Jed said grimly.

For a moment there was silence in the office.

'What's your plans now?' Lomax got up to stretch his legs. 'Still need a deputy or two. Unless you got someplace else to go.'

Jed thought for a moment. 'No, I ain't got anywhere better to go. Besides, I've got somebody to keep me here. Guess I'll ride up and see Jilly in the morning.'

This Large Print Book for the Partially sighted, who cannot read normal print, is published under the auspices of

THE ULVERSCROFT FOUNDATION

Other DALES Western Titles In Large Print

ELLIOT CONWAY
The Dude

JOHN KILGORE
Man From Cherokee Strip

J. T. EDSON
Buffalo Are Coming

ELLIOT LONG
Savage Land

HAL MORGAN
The Ghost Of Windy Ridge

NELSON NYE
Saddle Bow Slim